raising love

A FRIENDS-TO-LOVERS STORY

GREENE GARDENS COLLECTIVE

BROOKELYN MOSLEY

85 MEDIA LLC

Raising Love
Copyright © 2025 by Brookelyn Mosley

This book is a work of fiction. Names, characters, places, and incidents either are products of the author's imagination or are used fictitiously. Any resemblance to actual persons, living or dead, events, or locales is entirely coincidental.

ISBN (eBook): 978-1-965507-38-4

ISBN (Paperback): 978-1-965507-39-1

First Edition, 2025

Published by 85 Media LLC

Cover Design: Brookelyn Mosley/85 Media LLC

85 Media LLC

6614 Avenue U # 575

Brooklyn, NY 11234-6021

www.BrookelynMosley.com

bybk exclusives

Bed Bully

Stuck

LHR Rewind Series

Home Before Midnight

Maybe This Time Will Be Different

Lovekilla

Incoming Call

Rough

WYD

Drinks on Me

Cali & Lee

Ray & Jay

Living Out a Love Song

Glimpses

One Mic

With Love, Ayanna & Dallas

Just Friends

Lena's Ex-File

Dream Boss

Chateau Luxure

- Ready or Not

- So This is Love

- Home Before Midnight

- GLUTTONY

- When Luke Met Juliette

- When Life Gives You Sunsets

- In Love, I Trust

- Wrath

- Sloth

Short Stories

- Unsilent Knight

- Twice In Love

- Home For Christmas

message from the author

Thank you for purchasing your paperback copy of *Raising Love*. I'm excited for you to experience Ivy and Leo's story, which I poured my heart into from the first word to the last.

But first, a heads up. This book touches on grief and mourning as our characters figure out life and love after a huge loss. It's all written with care, like I always do, but if those themes are tough for you, just know they're there.

Raising Love is a standalone read. You can jump right in and get the full experience without any homework. But, if you're one of those folks who love a good Easter egg or exploring character connections, check out the Character Cameo page once you're done reading. It'll show you where else some of the side characters pop up in my other books, in case you're curious.

I hope you find Ivy and Leo's journey as magical and real as I did when writing it. They remind us that new beginnings can sprout from the most unexpected places.

Happy reading and much love,
Brookelyn.

acknowledgments

A loving thank you to my amazing husband who is without a doubt one of my biggest supporters. A special thank you to my reading family and early supporters of my work. I'm sure you've noticed the changes; you've even commented on it. I thank you for sticking beside me and growing with me. You all have embraced my brand of writing and I'm beyond appreciative of it. Shout out to the readers who have reached out to me to share your thoughts regarding my books. I thank you for keeping me motivated and excited to create new projects for you. When I write, I keep you in mind. Thank you for your support. It's my soul food.

ONE

ivy

BRONX, NEW YORK - DECEMBER 2024

I ADJUSTED my earpiece as I stood from my seat on the sidelines. The Ballers' basketball game had just ended, yet the arena was still alive with energy. Streamers continued to fall from overhead, and the crowd's cheers echoed around the vast arena as I made my way along the hardwood floor, my heels clicking beneath me.

Our eyes met as my friend Leo wrapped up another interview. I held up my microphone, emblazoned with the station's logo, to catch his attention, and he gestured for me to come over.

It was game day at the brand new Bronx Metro Arena, the Ballers' newly minted home as of this year. The Bronx Ballers, after a three-game losing streak, had finally claimed a victory over their opponents. Sometimes, I had to remind myself that I was on the sidelines for work, not just for fun. My voice was hoarse from all the shouting whenever I felt the referee made a questionable call—which was far too often.

"What the fuck was the ref's problem tonight?" I asked Leo as soon as I was within earshot. "You guys got beef or something?"

"I know, right?! Shit." He chuckled, towering over me. "Just riding my back all night like my initials were MTA."

1

Leo crouched down slightly to kiss me on the cheek, his sweat-slick lips brushing against my skin. I playfully pushed him away.

"Ew, LV. Come on," I protested, patting my foundation dry. "Don't mess up my makeup before I go on air."

He snickered. "How long is this gonna take, anyway." He lifted his arm to sniff his armpit. "I need a shower."

"It'll be quick," I told him. "Three questions max, like always. Cool?"

"Cool," he replied, pausing to dap one of his friends from the opposing team who passed by.

"You got lucky tonight," the player teased.

"Is that salt I'm smelling on your breath?" Leo retorted, and I giggled at their banter. "It's not good to be this salty. Too much salt isn't good for you, man."

"Ready when you are, Ivy," announced Jim, my camera operator, as he navigated through the crowd.

"Great," I nodded to Leo. "Ready?"

"Born ready, Ivy League," he replied, using the nickname I despised but secretly found endearing.

Jim counted us down silently with his fingers.

I quickly ran my fingers through my hair, making sure it stayed neatly in its bun, and smoothed down my blouse. "You better not call me Ivy League on air, you hear me? I'm not playing with you."

Leo laughed loudly.

"Three, two," Jim counted down, then pointed at us as he mouthed *one.*

"I'm Ivy Pressman, standing here with the man of the hour," I began, looking up at Leo. "The unstoppable Leo Vanguard, who killed it tonight with 12 assists and 5 blocks. It was almost unreal the amount of work this man put in on the court tonight, but don't worry, I won't let him steal all the glory, Ballers."

Leo laughed beside me.

"Another amazing game, Leo."

"Thank you, thank you," he said, his voice carrying over the crowd's noise.

"You're keeping up quite the record this season. Any secret moves you've been hiding from us, or is this just natural Vanguard talent?"

"I breathe this kind of effort as easily as I exhale air, Ivy." He smirked. "You know what's up."

"*Mm-hmm,*" I replied, playfully rolling my eyes. "I hear that, and I can't even knock you because it's justified. You did your thing tonight."

He bowed, exaggeratively.

"That last play got the crowd on their feet," I continued. "Did you plan that, or were you just in the zone?"

"I'm always in the zone, baby," Leo began. "It's easy to be when you're playing at home with fans as supportive as the Bronx Ballers'. The greatest fans in the country. I love hearing them cheer; it's as sweet to me as the sound of my heart beating."

"So, word is you've been stepping up as a real leader of the Ballers, alongside our guy Jaleel Gordon," I said, turning to face him fully. "With Pryce Williams now retired, how does it feel knowing the team looks up to you?"

"Kind of hard for them to look down when I'm one of the tallest dudes on this team, right, Ivy League?" he teased.

I gasped and glanced quickly at the camera, then back at Leo, moving in close enough to pinch him on the arm discreetly.

"Ow!" he quipped, trying to hold back his laughter. "For someone so little you pinch hard, man. Damn!"

"What did I tell you about calling me that?" I whispered fiercely.

Leo grabbed my wrist, pulling the mic closer. "Do y'all at home watching know she's mean?"

"Aht!" I protested, trying to pull away.

"This beauty is a beast and has a mean streak, so y'all keep that in mind when watching her," he continued, smirking into the camera. "Say the right thing all the time, or she'll pinch you."

I pushed him away, freeing my wrist, and he bent his knees to pull me close and planted a loud kiss on my cheek.

"*Ugh!*" I tried to hit him with my microphone, but he dodged, laughing along with Jim, who was struggling to keep the camera steady.

This was why my station's producer always sent me to games to interview Leo. Not only because we'd known each other for years since college but also because we always made viewers laugh with our antics.

Mostly Leo's antics, if I'm being real.

"Thank you for taking the time to talk to us, Leo," I said, barely concealing my irritation.

"Always, my love," he joked, his tone light.

"Shut up," I sneered, and even that made him laugh.

"Aye, *Free-Throw Nation*," Leo declared, looking directly into the camera. "Ivy Pressman is the Bronx Ballers' lucky charm. You have her to thank for tonight. You heard it from me first. Peace." Leo flashed a peace sign as he walked away from me and the camera, backwards.

"There you have it," I concluded for the viewers, finally letting my giggles show. "I'm Ivy Pressman, live here at the Bronx Metro Arena, where the Ballers have secured a win that will keep them in the running for the championships. Can they do it? I know they can."

"And cut," Jim said, lowering the camera from his shoulder with a smile. "I swear you two are magic on camera, Ivy."

"Please don't encourage his foolishness." I laughed, shaking my head. "Let's get out of here. My feet are killing me in these damn heels."

* * *

I sat at my desk in the co-working space I rented, staring at the computer screen with tired eyes. I had to blink a few times then bug my eyes out to keep awake. It was just after midnight, and in five hours, I would have been up for twenty-four. It was a chosen torture, the sacrifice needed to make my dreams a reality.

Since I was five years old, watching games with my maternal grandfather, I knew what I wanted to do. At the end of every game, someone was on the hardwood floor, mic in hand, asking players questions. Sports was our bonding activity, and when my grandfather passed away when I was eighteen, I knew I wanted to continue that legacy, which I am doing now at thirty.

"Do y'all at home watching know she's mean?" Leo's voice came from the screen.

"Aht!" I watched as I turned to face him on the playback.

I chuckled to myself. "He's such an ass," I murmured, my amusement clear.

Leo and I, along with our best friends Kendra, who I sometimes called Kenni, and Tyrell, had been inseparable since our freshman year in college. While Leo pursued NBA dreams, Tyrell became a high school basketball coach. Kendra and Tyrell were expecting, and their baby shower, which Leo and I had organized, was the upcoming weekend.

That's why I found myself editing videos in this overpriced co-working space at such a late hour. With the baby shower around the corner, I knew this might be my only chance to get the edits done.

Editing wasn't necessary, but I chose to do it for the experience. Besides, I had commentary to record for my YouTube channel. It doesn't have many followers yet, but it's my side hustle that earns me enough each month to buy at least two cups of good coffee.

Fighting off sleep, I slapped my cheeks and reached for my water bottle, standing to set up my camera and lighting. Despite needing rest for tomorrow's event, I was driven, fueled by the dream of making it big in sports journalism.

I placed my camera on the tripod, adjusting the lighting before sitting down to record.

"This is a test video," I announced to the camera, practicing a few smiles.

Because Leo was right—I tended to be a bit uptight. His nickname for me, 'Ivy League,' was a playful jab at that. I was constantly working not to let that side show too much, which was a personal battle.

After checking the playback, my phone rang, snapping me out of my focus.

"Who the hell is that?" I muttered, picking up the phone to see Kendra's name. I answered immediately.

"What's up, girl?" I greeted her. "Everything okay?"

"Damn." Kendra chuckled on the other end. "Can I get a hello first?"

"Not when you're calling after midnight," I retorted, sinking back into my chair. "What are you even doing up?"

"What are *you* doing up?" she shot back.

"Answering your call, obviously," I quipped.

She laughed loudly. "Well, I figured you'd be up. I was actually hoping you weren't."

I glanced at my camera setup, sighing. "Well, you know your best friend."

"*Mm-hmm,*" Kendra agreed. "I know she works too damn hard."

"There's no such thing," I countered.

"I caught a bit of you and Leo on air tonight after his game." She giggled. "I swear, I love seeing you two together."

I rolled my eyes. "He's a jackass."

"Oh, you love it!" Kendra teased.

"Anyway," I shifted the topic. "What's up?"

Kendra had tried to set Leo and me up during our first week as freshmen in college. She and Tyrell, Leo's best friend from high school, had recently started dating, and naturally, she attempted to match me with Tyrell's friend. It didn't take long to see that he wasn't for me. Leo was incessantly jovial, a class clown who rarely took things seriously. On our double date, he spent more time eyeing every woman that passed by than engaging in our conversation. By the end of the night, it was clear the feeling was mutual. Leo even started calling me 'Ivy League,' joking that having a conversation with me was as tough as getting into an Ivy League school.

Over the years, he started using that nickname as his way of saying *'obviously,'* always teasing me with a playful tone.

Still, that nickname was a bit of a trigger. I've always felt slightly out of place among my peers, though Kendra never made me feel that way. She treated me not just as a friend but as a sister.

"I was just calling to remind you about the baby shower," Kendra said.

"The one I organized and am hosting for you?" I replied, my tone playful.

She laughed. "I know you're swamped, and I just wanted to make sure you remember your dear friend."

"Nothing about you is 'little' anymore, Kenni."

She gasped playfully, and I chuckled. "I'm kidding... sort of."

When Kendra first told me she was pregnant, I thought it was a joke. The same went for her engagement. Now here she was, married, expecting, and moving into a house in Greene Gardens, the new village everyone in New York seemed to be talking about. Meanwhile, I was in a co-working space, red-eyed and scrambling up the career ladder at thirty.

It is what it is.

"And for the record, I'm never too busy for you or the baby... which you still haven't named, and you haven't even told me if it's a boy or a girl."

"I want it all to be a surprise," she insisted. "Even Tyrell and I don't know what we're having."

"Couldn't be me." I shook my head. "The mystery would drive me insane."

She chuckled.

"Do you at least have names picked out?"

"We have a name for each," she replied, her voice warm. "We'll share them when it's time. Just make sure you handle your godmother duties this weekend."

I cringed. "Godmother, Kenni? Are you sure about this?"

"Ivy, we're not having this conversation again," she said firmly.

"I just... I don't know the first thing about babies, Kenni. They're like little aliens to me."

"You'll learn," she assured me, her tone light.

"Hmph."

"Just don't forget this weekend," she added. "The invitations you sent out were adorable, by the way."

I smiled, feeling a flicker of pride. "Already being the best godmother ever, huh?"

"Exactly," Kendra agreed, laughing. "This weekend, then. I love you, girl."

"And I love you back."

leo

"OH, GOD. OH GOD!" Vanessa shouted in my ear, clinging tightly to my back. "Oh my God."

The silk sheets on my bed crinkled beneath us, emphasizing my movements as I moved in and out between Vanessa's clenching walls.

"Oh, baby, ohhhh, right there!"

"*Mmm-hmm*," I groaned, my body quivering over her as I guided us both through a slow-building climax.

I could feel her nails digging into my back like she was trying to claw out a mound of clay. The pain mixed with the pleasure, making me roar my release into the pillow beneath her head.

"Oh God, you're so good," she exhaled, then pressed her lips to my shoulder. "My goodness."

That was my name every time Vanessa and I spent time like this. God. I was her God, and I loved that shit so damn much.

I lifted myself just enough to roll off her and onto my pillow, but Vanessa gripped my back and wrapped her legs around my waist, keeping me in place.

"*Mmm*," she moaned, pressing another kiss into my shoulder. "Don't move."

I sighed out a laugh, putting in a little more effort to break free from her hold. I finally succeeded, rolling to my side and relaxing on my pillow, my eyes fixed on the ceiling as I caught my breath.

She was on me a second later—her leg, at least—as she draped it over my thigh.

I tried to keep my annoyance to myself.

Vanessa was a woman I met at a club during one of my paid appearances. She was Halle Berry in the '90s fine. Same short cut and all. Men in the club were damn near offering to pay her rent for the next five years when I spotted her in VIP, seeing no one but me, eyeing me like a bald eagle.

She was bold but still knew how to play it cool, which I liked. The thing I didn't like, though, was her penchant for being clingy. That night, and every other night for the past two summers, it showed.

She moved in closer, angling her lips toward my neck before shifting to kiss my lips.

"Damn, baby," I mumbled. "Can I catch my breath on my own for a minute?"

"No," she said through a moan, pecking another kiss against my lips. "Because whenever we're done, and I don't keep my hands on you like this, you leave."

I scoffed a laugh. "That is not true."

"What you're denying is what's not true," she said back.

My room looked every bit like the hookup we just had: wild and disorderly. Clothes were strewn here and there, sheets disheveled under the dim morning light filtering through my slightly opened curtains.

"Want to grab breakfast?" she asked, her voice soft against me.

"*Hmmm*," I started, "I actually have somewhere I have to be in a couple of hours."

"See?" she said, sitting up and snatching my bedding to cover her breasts.

I sat up too. "See, what?"

"Leo, every time we hook up, you conveniently have somewhere to be right after."

She wasn't completely wrong. Last night when Vanessa called me to hang out, I didn't decline. I knew I had my friend Tyrell and his wife Kendra's baby shower to attend today, but I still said Vanessa could swing by... because I knew I'd have an event to run off to.

Women be knowing. Because how Vanessa knew I was running off soon after hooking up was beyond me.

Vanessa was a beautiful and accomplished woman, working as a personal stylist for some of the most notable politicians around New York City. I met her in her hometown of Atlanta two years ago, when I visited one of their clubs after a game. I was there for a paid appearance.

She relocated to New York shortly after we met and has been here since. At night, at the clubs, she knew how to let her hair down as a socialite. She was fun, but I simply didn't see this thing we had going on being more than fun.

I kicked my legs off the bed and reached for my boxers—one of the strewn garments on the floor. "I have a baby shower to go to this afternoon."

She kissed her teeth.

"It's been planned for months. I'm one of the hosts."

"If you knew you had somewhere to be today," she started, "why didn't you tell me that when I asked if I could come over to spend the weekend, Leo?"

"Because..." I shrugged. "I didn't think you meant the whole weekend."

"I sure as hell didn't mean a night, Leo!"

"Okay." I held a hand up. "Aight, I apologize for not keeping it real with you and letting you know I had plans for today, okay?"

"No, it's not okay," she argued, turning more to face me. "You do this all the time—"

Our back and forth was interrupted by my phone ringing. I turned to see Ivy's name sprawled across the screen.

Vanessa saw it too, expressing her annoyance by kissing her teeth. "And now this bullshit."

"What's up, Ivy League?" I said, answering the phone.

Ivy sighed on the other end. "I really hate when you call me that."

I chuckled, my gaze lifting long enough to see Vanessa scowling on my bed, her eyes locked on me in a death stare.

"Uh..." I turned away from her glare. "What's up?"

"Can you pick me up a little earlier than we discussed?" Ivy asked. "The cake is ready for pickup, and I'd feel a lot better if we got it now instead of later."

I smirked. "What could possibly happen if we got the cake at the time we agreed on?"

"You mean the time *you* told me would be the best, even though I said it wasn't? The time I didn't really want to go with in the first place, but gave in to avoid going back and forth with you? That time, Leo?"

I snickered while shaking my head.

Vanessa cleared her throat behind me.

When I turned to look her way, she rolled her eyes and snapped her neck. "Were you not doing something?"

"Aight, cool," I said into the phone, eyes still on Vanessa. "I'll be there in an hour."

Vanessa sucked her teeth so loud.

"Be here in half an hour," Ivy said back.

Ivy. Always so damn extra.

After a really bad first date and double date we'd gone on with our friends, Ivy and I decided we'd do better as friends—and we did. We had a lot in common. Both lovers of sports, we connected over shit-talking and placing bets on games.

And while we had a friendly rivalry, Ivy was one of the most supportive people in my life. She'd been at every home game of my career, from college to now. These days, she'd often shout at refs from the sideline, completely forgetting she was working.

I loved that the most about my little homie.

"Half an hour?" I laughed. "Didn't I just say I just got up?"

"Not my problem," she sang into the phone. I just knew she was wearing one of her little smirks. "See you in half an hour."

"Ivy—"

Before I could protest anything else, she hung up the phone.

I laughed to myself while removing the phone from my ear. "This woman is a trip."

I turned to see Vanessa staring me down from her spot on my bed. For a split second, I had honestly forgotten she was still here.

"Welcome back, after your visit to cloud nine," she said, balling her lips right after her words left her mouth.

"Vanessa, chill."

"Chill?!" She kicked her legs off the bed. The moment she was on her feet, she walked my way. "I just watched my boyfriend light up while talking to another woman."

"Whoa." I held a hand up in front of me. "I am not your boyfriend."

"Why is that, Leo? *Hmmm*?" Vanessa folded her arms over her chest. "We have been dating each other for two years now."

I shook my head. "We have not been dating."

She scoffed.

"Look, Vanessa," I started. "You can say what you want about me, but you can't say I've been leading you on. I've told you from the start, relationships are not my thing, baby. My career is. So…"

She kissed her teeth.

"While I respect your feelings, let's maintain an air of honesty about what we've got going on, aight?"

"Which is?"

I glanced over at her.

"What are we, Leo?" she quizzed. "Because I swear I see you show more affection to your friend than you actually do the girl you're fucking. Unless you're fucking Ivy too."

I snorted a laugh, which turned into a bellyful chuckle. "Yeah, aight. I assure you that fucking ain't happening with Ivy and me. At all."

"Well, the way you talk to her sure makes it seem like you want to."

"Ha!"

"And the way she *loves* talking to you," Vanessa continued, "I wouldn't be surprised if she wants to, too."

"Aight, enough." I clapped my hands once. "Like I told you, Vanessa, I gotta go, baby." I approached her, bending my knees to be at her level. "While I would love to go back and forth with you—because you look so damn beautiful when you're pissed at me…"

She tried to fight her smile but couldn't resist, rolling her eyes and looking away instead.

"As you heard, I have to go." I pressed a kiss against her forehead before turning away and heading to my bathroom. "I gotta hop in the shower." I glanced at her over my shoulder. "You're more than welcome to join me."

Her face lit up.

"But we gotta make it quick," I informed her. "I'm not trying to have Ivy waiting."

Vanessa's smile melted right off her face. "No thank you, then."

My smile faded too, but I didn't let myself stay in that feeling.

It's like I said: Ivy was a punctual and by-the-book kind of woman. She was cool, but she didn't play with the things she was responsible for. I respected that, and I respected her.

And despite Vanessa's feelings about my relationship with Ivy, she and I were never—and could never be—what Vanessa suggested we were.

I shook my head while snickering. "Just trippin'," I said as I turned the knob on my shower's stall, watching as water spilled out overhead. "As if Ivy and I could ever."

THE SUDDEN, loud chime of my phone on the night table beside my bed jolted me out of sleep. While the call woke me, it took a minute to register that my phone was ringing.

My eyes scanned the ceiling as the chiming continued—until it stopped. Less than a second later, the device started chiming again.

Something about the call coming in twice had me sitting up instantly, reaching for my phone and answering before even checking who it was.

Before I could say anything, Leo spoke.

"Ivy."

I moved the phone away from my ear and glanced at the screen, searching for the time. It was two in the morning. No good calls came in at two in the morning.

Aside from that, it was the way my friend said my name—slowly, weighted with something my tired brain couldn't quite decipher. But I knew it wasn't good.

"Leo?"

"There's been an accident," he revealed.

"Huh?"

"I'm... I'm at Brooklyn Bay Medical Center."

I blinked erratically, the words not fully registering. "What? Are you okay?"

"It's Kenni and Rell, man," he said low, inhaling a deep breath after.

My heart felt like it stopped in my chest. My stomach knotted less than a second later.

"Kendra *and* Tyrell?"

"To Kendra and Tyrell," I'd said in front of my best friend and her husband, holding up a glass of mimosa. "May your mommy and daddy years be your best years yet."

Everyone cheered behind me, making me smile even wider as I raised my glass along with the rest. I grinned behind the rim as I took a sip.

Kendra's baby shower had been a hit. Everything went as planned and without a hitch, just the way I liked it. Making sure we got the cake ahead of time and checking on the hall before the shower began had been excellent planning and execution. I was starting off this godmother gig pretty well.

"Okay, girl," Kendra said as she waddled up to me, pulling me into a tight hug. I held her just as tightly back, leaving enough room between us for her belly. "You did that!"

I tossed my head back in a laugh. "Did you like it?"

"Liked it?" Kendra grinned. "This is the best baby shower I've ever attended—and I've been to too many."

I giggled. "This was my first one, so I was a little worried—"

"You did great." She nodded. "You worry too much."

"Worry too much, work too much, avoid men too much," I listed, recalling all the things she'd always told me. "Did I get them all?"

She kissed her teeth. "I'm not even getting into it with you."

I snickered.

"Ready, baby?" Tyrell, Kendra's husband and Leo's best friend, said as he approached. He wrapped his arm around her, resting his hand on her belly. "We want to get on the road ahead of traffic."

I glanced out the window at the view of New York City through the thick pane glass. Flurries were starting to fall, resembling sprinkles of sugar drifting from the sky.

I pointed toward the window. "Y'all sure you want to drive all the way upstate today? It looks like it's starting to snow, and the newscasters have been saying this is going to be a big storm."

Tyrell tightened his arm around Kendra. "I tried to tell her, but she insists on this damn baby moon."

I looked at her and shook my head.

"And whatever my big baby wants, she gets," he added with a smile.

I sighed, glancing out the window again, my brows furrowing the longer I watched the flurries.

"We'll be fine," Kendra offered. "There you go worrying again over nothing."

I rolled my eyes, turning back to face them.

"This baby will be here in two weeks," she reminded. "I want to enjoy as much of my free time as I can. I need this baby moon with my man."

Tyrell leaned forward to press a kiss to Kendra's cheek.

These two had been annoyingly cute from the start of their relationship in college. Almost made me want one of those "things"—but I knew better. I worked a lot, but at least my work yielded results that made my life better. Dating, on the other hand... I couldn't say the same.

"Speaking of the baby being here in two weeks," Leo said, approaching us from behind me, "can we get a name now?"

Kendra and Tyrell looked at each other before laughing.

"For real," I added, folding my arms. "Why do the godparents have to wait like everyone else to find out their godchild's name?"

"Because we want it to be a surprise, so hush," Kendra stated. "And no more about it. In two weeks, you'll not only find out if it's a boy or girl, but you'll also find out the name in due time. Patience people."

I was in my car and headed to the medical center in no time. I didn't bother getting presentable—no makeup, none of it. I didn't do any of the things I insisted on doing when preparing to face the world. I still had my bonnet on my head, throwing on a white tee and jeans beneath my cold-weather coat.

All I could think about was getting out of my apartment as fast as I could and to the medical center.

Kendra and Tyrell. What the hell happened?

Waiting at every red light was torture. My heart wouldn't stop racing, replaying the last time I saw my best friend and her husband. The big, bright smiles they both wore. How Tyrell couldn't keep his hand off her belly.

"The baby," I whispered to myself.

The driver behind me honked their horn, and my eyes shot up to the traffic light—it had changed from red to green.

I exhaled as I stepped on the gas, resuming my drive.

The cold night was unforgiving. The flurries from earlier, once light and harmless, now fell rapidly, sticking to the asphalt and sidewalks. I could barely see through it.

"Are they okay?" I asked Leo over the phone.

"Just get here, Ivy, please," he replied. "I don't want to do this over the phone."

Although Leo refused to tell me more, I felt like I already knew the answer to my question. My hands could barely steady on the steering wheel, gripping the leather to keep my whole body from shaking with pure anxiety.

Tears streamed down my face by the time I arrived at the medical center's parking lot.

Leo wasn't his usual playful self over the phone. I'd never heard him sound so serious—and something else. There was something in his voice that told me everything I needed to know, though part of me refused to accept it.

Out of my car and in front of the medical center's doors, I spotted Leo through the turnstile glass, his head in his hands.

My heart sank immediately. Any confidence I had that everything would be fine sank with it, deep into the pit of my stomach.

"Leo," I said the moment I stepped inside.

And the second he lifted his face, I felt a pang in my stomach.

The food I had eaten earlier in the night pushed up quickly.

I slapped my hand to my mouth, forcing the bile down and trying to catch the scream—then the cry—that boomed out of me anyway, just like the tears in my eyes.

The shaking in my hands returned, and with nothing to grip for comfort, my whole body started trembling violently. I couldn't stop it, no matter how much I wanted to.

Hands, then arms, engulfed me. That was the only thing I could feel in that moment.

Leo had wrapped his arms around me, guiding my face into his chest and holding it there with gentle tension.

"You gotta calm down, Ivy," he whispered against me.

"Please tell me they're fine, LV," I whispered back. "Please just tell me that."

He didn't say anything in response, but I felt the motion of his head moving from side to side, indicating his answer was no.

That made my legs lose what little strength they had left. He caught me, holding me up.

* * *

"What the hell happened?" I asked in a whisper, seated across from him.

The doctors and nurses had been kind enough to let Leo and me sit in one of their meeting rooms in the medical center's lobby.

After I'd became inconsolable in the main entrance, likely worrying everyone at that hour, they offered us somewhere private where I could collect myself.

After a few more minutes of bawling my eyes out when Leo confirmed Kendra and Tyrell were gone, my investigative mind kicked in. I needed the information.

"There was a pile-up on the I-87," Leo rasped before clearing his throat. "It's all over the news."

I blinked rapidly, trying to keep the tears in my eyes.

Leo inhaled deeply. "Kendra and Tyrell were on their way

upstate. A driver lost control of their car. The police said the driver hit ice beneath the snow, spun out, and lost control. Kendra and Tyrell were right behind them, and…"

He cleared his throat. "Other cars started slowing down, but it was too late. The others… they started losing control too. Kendra and Tyrell's car got hit a couple of times." Leo shook his head, gesturing behind him with his hand. "Their car got hit from the back, the side. They said they had to use the jaws of life to pry it open because… Kendra and Tyrell were trapped inside."

"Oh my God." I pressed my fingers to my eyes.

"It took a minute for emergency vehicles to get to them because of the snow and the pile-up."

I started crying again, unable to hold it in.

"Come on, Ivy, please," Leo said softly, his tone unlike any I'd ever heard him use with me. "Please don't do that right now."

I forced myself to sniff my tears back.

"I know I'm asking for a lot, but I need you to be strong right now," he added. "Please."

I lifted my eyes to his and saw his emotions all over his face, though not a single tear escaped.

He'd lost a friend too. One he'd known for longer than I'd known Kendra. Leo and Tyrell had a brotherhood that was enviable, a bond that went deeper than friendship. They genuinely loved each other like brothers.

I reached across the table and took his hand, holding it tightly as I nodded and dropped my head to gather myself.

Then my head popped up again, and I damn near jumped out of my seat when the thought occurred.

"What happened to the baby?" I was out of my seat a second later. "Oh God, what happened to the baby?"

"They're fine," Leo told me. "In the NICU. Doctors delivered the baby via c-section after they… got Kendra out." He nodded. "The baby's in the NICU for observation and care."

"How do you know all of this?"

He scoffed a laugh. "A very talkative nurse who's also a Bronx Ballers fan was generous with the info. Plus, Tyrell's mom and Kendra's parents confirmed the baby is fine."

I sat back down. "Are they here?"

"Tyrell's mom had to be carried out shortly before you arrived," he said, shaking his head slowly. "They had to give her oxygen because she couldn't breathe when she got the news. And she just had surgery." Leo shook his head. "A family member came to get her soon after, and everyone agreed it was best for her to leave. Kendra's parents are still here, though."

"Their parents..." I sighed heavily. "I'm over here making a big deal about this, thinking about me, and I didn't even consider their parents."

Leo dropped his head, running a hand down his face.

"Kendra's parents just retired and moved out of their house and into a one-bedroom apartment, and Tyrell's mom recently had hip replacement surgery. Fuck." I shook my head, staring at the wall behind Leo. "This is really fucked up."

* * *

Leo and I spent a few more minutes in the meeting room before deciding to take the elevator to the NICU.

The whole way up felt surreal. I didn't even feel like I was actually doing anything—walking, scanning with my eyes, or hearing the faint hum of the hospital around me. Everything felt muted and distant. The beeping of machines, murmured voices, the lingering medicinal smells—it all combined to create a place nobody would willingly choose to be.

The hospital staff wouldn't let Leo and me into the NICU, which was expected, but it didn't help my inner panic.

What if the baby *isn't* okay?

I knew we likely wouldn't be allowed in, but I had to try.

When we arrived on the floor, Kendra's parents were already

there, visibly shaken and grieving.

Though we couldn't enter the NICU, I could see the general layout of the unit through the viewing window. The lighting was softer than the rest of the hospital, and the incubators were spread out at a distance, making it hard to tell which one held Kendra and Tyrell's baby.

I hugged Kendra's parents separately, her father putting up a strong facade while her mother cried against me. Her grief forced me to stay strong.

"How's the baby?" I asked the moment I could.

"He's... beautiful," Mrs. Simmons said, her bottom lip trembling. "I haven't seen his eyes yet, but... *uh*..." She inhaled deeply. "The shape of them? It's all Kendra."

"He," I repeated, a small smile pulling at my lips. "It's a boy."

"A boy," Mr. Simmons exhaled, looking up at the ceiling as if to hold his tears back.

"Kendra swore it was a girl," I said, my slight giggle morphing into a weighted sigh as I ran a hand down my face. I glanced at Leo, leaning against the wall behind us, his eyes cast down at the floor.

He hadn't shed a tear, but his eyes looked like he'd been crying for hours.

"They won't let us see him," I told the Simmons. "Which... I guess I understand why."

"I took a picture," Mrs. Simmons said softly, pulling out her phone and thumbing in her password. "They told us it was okay."

That got Leo off the wall and heading in our direction.

The first thing I noticed in the picture was how tiny Kendra and Tyrell's son was, his delicate features framed by the medical equipment that underscored both his vulnerability and strength.

"What are all these things on him?" I asked, pointing at the IV line in his arms and legs and the tube in his nose. "Is he okay? Was he hurt?"

Mrs. Simmons nodded quickly. "He's fine. He's... great, actually. Full-term, due only in two weeks, so..." She paused to nod while dabbing her eyes with her fingers. "He was developed enough to survive outside of the womb." She swallowed hard and blinked back the rest of her tears. "The wires and tubes, it's just... it's protocol. Preventative care, according to the NICU nurse."

And aside from all the wires and tubes, he was beautiful. Laying there in a clear plastic enclosure and on what looked to be soft bedding. He looked so small.

I swallowed back the cry I could feel forming in my throat as a knot and exhaled a stuttered breath.

"I know," Mrs. Simmons said, her voice breaking as her eyes filled with tears. "I know."

I drew her into another hug, holding her tightly while forcing back my tears by holding my breath.

We all spent a few more minutes on the NICU floor before deciding to leave and return the next day.

I had no idea what tomorrow would bring. This was all so crazy and too sudden.

In situations like this, I always thought that I would get to a quiet space—often back at home, pull out my phone, and dial up Kendra, starting our conversation with, "Girl, let me tell you what happened." But I couldn't do that now. I would never be able to do that ever again. Because Kendra was what happened. My best friend was gone.

Leo walked me to my car in the parking lot, the both of us silent. The only sounds were those of our footwear tapping along the asphalt.

"I'm so tired," I said as I pulled out my key fob. "But I have no idea how I'm going to be able to go back to sleep."

"Tell me about it," he replied.

The redness in his eyes had subsided, though it seemed even more pronounced against his light brown skin.

I was sure my eyes looked no better. Leo and I were the same light brown complexion, and grief had clearly painted its toll on both of us.

"Did you park in the lot?" I asked.

"I took a cab here," he revealed. "I was at the club when I got the call. Too drunk to get into any car to drive."

We stared at each other for a moment, my chin quivering as the reality of the night finally started to settle in.

"I can't believe they're gone, Leo," I whispered, unable to contain the weight of the truth any longer. "Like, I am literally having a hard time accepting that our friends are gone. Just like that."

Before a single tear could fall from my eyes, Leo stepped into my space without hesitation and wrapped his arms tightly around me, holding me close.

And I let it all out—every ounce of whatever I was feeling that made the air impossible to breathe and the truth that my best friend... no, my sister, was really gone.

leo

OUR FOOTSTEPS ECHOED as we made our way down the long, narrow corridor.

"And here we are," Carla, the woman who greeted Ivy and me when we arrived, said as she gestured into the office. "Mr. Grant will be with you shortly. Can I get you two anything?"

I shook my head in response as I entered and took a seat.

"We're fine," Ivy said, trailing behind me. "Thank you."

The last four days had been a blur—a literal lapse in time that seemed to happen completely out of my control. I hadn't slept right since getting the news. Every time my phone rang after a certain hour, my heart would jolt in my chest.

Ivy sighed as she slumped in her chair beside me.

Neither one of us had been okay. I had a game the day after getting the news about Tyrell and Kendra. I played like shit, which was to be expected. Instead of my coach getting at me for my terrible performance on the court, the man just hugged me after the game in the locker room.

Everyone I knew, both professionally and personally, had been very understanding. And while the sympathy was appreciated, the only person I felt truly understood what I was going through was the woman sitting silently beside me, her shoulders slumped in her chair.

For the past four days, she and I had spoken on the phone for hours—sometimes saying nothing, just sitting in silence and listening to each other breathe. That simple sign of life had become a source of comfort for me.

I still couldn't believe this had happened. My boy, Tyrell, gone. Just like that.

"Good morning," a gentleman said behind us as he entered the office. "I'm Mr. Grant. I hope you weren't waiting long."

Ivy and I both sat up in our seats.

We'd gotten a strange phone call the day before—first her, then me. It was from a woman who identified herself as Carla Carey, the same woman who walked us into the office. She'd called to ask for our availability to meet with Kendra and Tyrell's estate lawyer.

I had no idea they even had an estate lawyer.

I was pressing my hands into the arms of the chair when Mr. Grant held up a hand. "Please, Mr. Vanguard, you don't need to get up."

The phone call had been to set up a meeting for the reading of Kendra and Tyrell's last will and testament with Mr. Grant.

"Very nice to meet you two," Mr. Grant said, extending his hand first to me, then to Ivy. We both shook it in turn. "I'm sorry we are meeting under these circumstances, but I'm happy you were able to meet me on such short notice. My condolences for your loss. Sincerely. I've known Kendra all her life, having also managed her parents' estate. And Tyrell seemed like a great guy as well."

"Thank you," Ivy replied. "Kendra and Tyrell were great. The best." She glanced at me briefly before turning back to Mr. Grant as he took a seat across from us at his desk. "I think I speak for both of us, though, when I say I have no idea why we are here."

"Oh." Mr. Grant wrinkled his bushy brows. "Did my assistant Carla not detail to you—"

"Oh, no." Ivy held up a hand. "She did. She explained that today's meeting would be for the reading of our friends' wills, but I'm not understanding why *we* are here and not their parents."

"Yeah," I concurred. "Although Ivy and I are like family to Kendra and Tyrell, we aren't actual family."

"The meeting with their parents occurred yesterday," Mr. Grant informed.

That made me tilt my head slightly.

"This reading of the will and testament is specifically for you two," he revealed. "Only you two."

"Really?" Ivy quizzed.

"Yes," Mr. Grant replied, his attention lowering to the filing folder he'd brought into the office.

The door opened a second later, and Carla stepped in holding a similar folder.

"As you know, this is Carla, my assistant," Mr. Grant said. "She'll be present during the reading and will handle document management."

Ivy and I glanced at each other before focusing back on Mr. Grant.

There was so much unknown, and the mystery was starting to make me lightheaded. I knew we were here for a will reading—something I'd never attended in my life. But a will reading for what? What could Kendra and Tyrell be leaving us?

When the call came in from Carla, I called Ivy immediately, and she confirmed receiving the same phone call. Nothing had been disclosed regarding why our attendance was necessary, but still, we showed up—because it was for our friends.

"First, I want to thank you two for coming in today," Mr. Grant started. "I know this must be a difficult time for both of you. I'll do my best to explain everything clearly so you understand what your friends, Kendra and Tyrell, have outlined in their will regarding your roles."

Roles? What roles?

"So, let's get started." Mr. Grant smiled politely, pushing back his large glasses up the bridge of his nose. "We're here today to discuss the last will and testament of Kendra and Tyrell Love, as you both know. Before we begin, I want to ensure you both understand the terms we will use and what they imply. Please feel free to stop me at any time with questions."

My heart started to thump in that instant.

Mr. Grant pulled out a document from the folder and fixed his attention on it. "This document I'm holding—and that I will show to you shortly—is legally binding and was drafted according to Kendra and Tyrell's instructions. To start, they have named both of you as guardians of their child, should anything happen to them."

Guardians? What does that mean?

I blinked rapidly, unable to process what I was hearing. It still hadn't registered.

"They have also left you their home in Greene Gardens," Mr. Grant continued, "which they intended to be a family home for them and their child."

"Wait, I'm sorry," Ivy exhaled, pressing her hand to her chest. "Perhaps I'm missing something. What do you mean they've named us guardians? Like, what *exactly* do you mean?"

Mr. Grant lifted his eyes to Ivy.

"I know Kendra wanted us to be godparents," Ivy informed. "Are guardians godparents, or...?"

"No, a guardian has more rights than a godparent," Mr. Grant explained. "I can clarify if you like."

"Yes." I nodded. "Please do."

"Sure," he said. "I'll outline what guardianship entails—not just in the immediate future, but long-term."

Long-term?

"Accepting guardianship of a child is akin to stepping into the role of a parent."

"Parent?" Ivy quizzed.

"Yes," Mr. Grant replied. "You'll be responsible for making all decisions concerning his health, education, and general welfare."

"Like parents," I said, more to myself. My eyes scanned the space around me, Mr. Grant's words sinking in and weighing on the panic slowly rising within me.

"Oh, shit," Ivy uttered, slapping her hand to her mouth. "I'm sorry."

Mr. Grant chuckled. "It's fine."

"Does it really say that?" Ivy asked, scooting to the edge of her seat and pointing at the document in Mr. Grant's hand. "Does it literally say they are leaving their actual human child with us?"

"Yes," Mr. Grant replied with a nod.

"They really didn't have anyone else in mind?" I asked. "Their parents? Other family?"

"People who know what to do with babies?" Ivy added, her exhales becoming audible beside me. "Because I assure you, that is *not* us."

"They were very specific in wanting you two. It seems they trusted you to provide the care and love their son would need."

"Why in the fuck...?!" Ivy's voice echoed around the room before she slapped her hand to her mouth again, only to remove it a second later to press against her chest. "Okay... um... legally. What does being a guardian look like, *legally*? Are we talking about something temporary, or...?"

"He said long-term, Ivy League," I interjected, hoping to lighten the moment—or at least myself. I was one inhale away from passing the hell out.

"Not right now," Ivy said, whipping her head in my direction. "Now is not the time for that shit, Leo."

"Guardianship is indeed a legal commitment, but not just temporary," Mr. Grant clarified. "Think of it as permanent—much like parenthood."

"There goes that *parent* word again," Ivy muttered, slumping back into her chair.

"You would be his legal guardians until he reaches adulthood or until the court deems otherwise. Should you choose to accept, I'll file a petition for guardianship with the family court. This process will officially recognize you as his legal guardians and grant you all parental rights."

"I'm gonna pass out," Ivy acknowledged, nodding her head as her hands shook. She lifted them to her head, as if trying to get a grip. "I'm gonna fucking pass out."

I couldn't even compose her because my ass was freaking out more than what she was showing. Everything was happening so damn fast. Why would Tyrell not tell me this was what he and Kendra planned in the unlikely event of their passing? Most importantly, why the hell would they leave their baby with Ivy and me of all people?

"There's no way they would trust us with this." Ivy shook her head incessantly. "Absolutely no way. I don't know the first thing about caring for and loving a child, and Leo over here..." She laughed nervously, glancing at me. "Leo." Ivy started waving her hand in the air and gesturing toward Mr. Grant. "Tell him how horrible we are. Tell him!"

I grimaced. "I wouldn't go as far as to say horrible."

Ivy placed her hand at the top of her head, going from sitting back to moving to the edge of her seat again. She never could keep her anxiety concealed.

"Kendra and Tyrell had the utmost confidence you two would manage this responsibility," Mr. Grant assured.

Ivy and I both focused on him.

He nodded. "It's a big responsibility. I get it. I have four children of my own, and not one of them was a cakewalk to raise. But Kendra and Tyrell insisted it be the both of you, and they've set aside a trust fund for the baby, which you'll manage for his needs."

I threw myself against the back of the chair and dropped my head into my hands.

This is not happening right now.

"I'm just not understanding why they wouldn't choose their family for this," Ivy expressed. "Why not their parents, who would know exactly what to do here? Isn't family the only people who could be guardians?"

"Guardianship isn't limited to family members," Mr. Grant said. "Friends can be appointed if parents believe they are the best choice. Your friends made this decision with a lot of thought, I assure you. When we drafted their will, they were thoughtful and deliberate about every detail. They spent two days deciding on guardianship. They wanted you two."

Ivy and I glanced at each other and held our stares.

All the color had drained from Ivy's russet brown skin. I was pretty sure I looked just as pale.

"They entrusted you with their most precious responsibility, and that decision wasn't made lightly," Mr. Grant continued. "And legally, this document I'm holding gives you the authority to act as parents would."

"Wow," I exhaled, emptying all the air I had with that word as I dropped my head forward and into my hands.

Ivy let out an audible breath and ran her hand down her face. "What kind of legal steps do we need to take now?"

"What?" I popped my head up out of my hands. "Ivy."

"What?" She focused on me.

"You can't be serious," I said low, even though it didn't matter who heard us.

"We should at least know how this will all work." Her chin began to quiver, her eyes filling with tears. "No?"

"Well, first," Mr. Grant started, waiting for our attention to return to him, "you'll need to formally accept the guardianship. We can take care of the paperwork today if you're ready."

I shut my eyes and held them tightly closed.

My heart was racing so fast at this point—faster than any moment on the court while trying to block a shot. Sometimes the block was successful; other times, a failure. And that was okay. I could learn from the failure and do better in the next game.

But that was a game. This was not.

"Babies are expensive," Ivy muttered. "I make a good living, but that's just for me. My apartment is small as hell—"

"There are also forms here to transfer the property in Greene Gardens into your names, as I mentioned," Mr. Grant interjected. "Kendra and Tyrell set up a trust fund for their baby, which you both will manage. The funds will cover his daily expenses, healthcare, education, and other needs. Detailed instructions and stipulations are outlined here," he added, gesturing at the document now lying on the table.

"I cannot believe they did all of this and told us nothing," Ivy muttered.

I swallowed the knot in my throat and straightened my back in my seat. "And if we find this isn't something we can handle?"

There was silence in the office for a beat.

"Yeah," Ivy finally said. "If we decide… I mean, if we *find* that we can't do this, what then?"

Mr. Grant shut his eyes and tilted his head forward, inhaling a deep breath. "It's a significant commitment; there's no question about that. If, after some consideration, you feel you cannot fulfill this role, we can petition the court for a reassignment of guardianship. However, such changes are generally seen as a last resort. I advise you to consider all factors seriously and possibly seek counseling to help with this transition."

I turned to meet Ivy's gaze, finding her head lowered and her eyes focused on her manicured nails. She appeared to be visibly digesting the information, her fingers tapping against her lap.

"Why don't we take a short break, yeah?" Mr. Grant suggested with a nod. He glanced behind us at Carla and raised a brow before focusing back on us. "I can prepare the initial paperwork, and you two can have a moment to discuss privately. We can reconvene in, say, fifteen minutes? Or if you feel you need more time to think outside of this office, the most I can offer is to reschedule our meeting for twenty-four hours from now."

I pressed my hand to my mouth and slowly ran my palm down

my beard. I never understood what people meant when they said they felt the walls were closing in during their times of panic. I found out exactly what they meant that day.

Because not even twenty-four hours seemed like enough time to decide what to do here.

A baby? Parents? What?!

I didn't know the first thing about babies. I was an only child. I grew up in a loving household, but shit, I always had my freedom. I never had to babysit anyone. I had no experience in this area—like, at all. There was no way I would be able to take care of a baby. No way.

Babies hadn't been on my radar. I thought Tyrell was crazy when he said that he and Kendra were purposefully working on having one shortly after they got married.

To me, children were little beings that consumed time and energy. I'd made up my mind years ago that they weren't for me. And now here I was, about to inherit one?

Shit.

"Can we get longer than twenty-four hours?" Ivy inquired.

Mr. Grant sucked in air through his teeth. "The thing is, Kendra and Tyrell's son has been in the NICU for four days already, which is fine because he's still under observation. He was delivered via c-section and with no health issues, so the monitoring was simply precautionary."

Mr. Grant lifted the document he'd been reading, placed it into the folder he walked in with, and closed it, folding his hands over it. "He is feeding well and has been ready for discharge for a few days now, but given the circumstances, the hospital's social services department has been coordinating with my office to understand the timeline for guardianship. He could go home as soon as today, which is what the hospital would prefer since he is feeding and growing appropriately. Keeping him there longer would present a problem. So, with this in mind, twenty-four hours to make a decision would be ideal and reasonable in this scenario."

Ivy and I glanced at each other.

"I have to make copies of one of these documents to give to you." Mr. Grant rolled his chair back on its wheels. "I'll give you two a few minutes to discuss timing, and when I return, you can tell me what you two want to do."

Ivy and I were left alone shortly after, our attention on everything but each other.

"What the entire fuck is happening right now?" she whispered, and I wasn't sure if she was asking herself or me.

The biggest decisions I'd had to make in life were what college to play for and whether to enter the NBA draft. I thought that was as hard as life would get for me. I never expected *this*. Losing a best friend, and him leaving me his baby? This was insane.

I squeezed my eyes closed and lifted my fingers to pinch the bridge of my nose, trying to calm the headache building.

"What are you thinking?" Ivy asked.

"I'm thinking... what the hell were Kendra and Tyrell on when they named us guardians, and how can I get that drug too? Because I sure could use it right now."

Ivy stared at me for a beat before snorting a laugh, which turned into a giggle. I couldn't resist laughing in response.

After a while, we were quiet again, and Ivy sighed as she leaned back in her seat. "This is all so damn sudden and crazy. Us? Why would they choose *us*?"

I blew air through my lips. "Questions that need answers."

Ivy sighed. "But who else does their baby have?"

"Their grandparents." I sat up in my seat and turned to face her. "Somebody else. Shit, *anyone* else."

Ivy nodded in agreement but then started shaking her head. "Let's just think about it."

"Think about it?"

"Yes." She nodded, her eyes scanning mine. "Let's take the twenty-four-hour break Mr. Grant mentioned to think about it and decide."

A part of me wanted to push back on even that. I was pretty sure that not even twenty-four hours would be enough time to decide if I wanted to take on the responsibility of raising a child.

Because essentially, that was what Ivy and I were being tasked with—raising a damn baby.

I released a heavy sigh and forced myself to nod anyway. "Aight, whatever. Let's take twenty-four."

* * *

"How about next week?" Vanessa asked in my ear.

Just the mention of the following week sent a pang to my gut as I pulled open the restaurant door. The entire reason I'd even taken her call was to distract myself from thinking about next week. Shit, distract me from thinking about right now.

I stepped inside and into a quieter atmosphere filled with soft jazz and murmurs around the room.

"Next week is the funeral for my friends," I mumbled as I greeted the hostess with a nod.

"Oh, shit," Vanessa whispered. "I'm sorry."

"It's cool," I assured. My attention moved to the hostess. "My party is already here. Ivy Pressman."

"Oh," Vanessa said into my ear. "You're... meeting up with Ivy?"

"This way, please," the hostess said with a smile, gesturing with her arm for me to follow her.

"Yeah," I said to Vanessa. "We're meeting up to discuss something."

"Like?" Vanessa pushed.

I sighed. "Not right now, Vanessa. Please."

She released a weighted exhale into the phone, making my eardrum vibrate.

The restaurant, Gotham Grill, was quiet at this hour. Only a few people sat at tables spaced out from one another. They spoke low, their voices blending into whispers beneath the soft music playing.

The lights were dim, and each table held a cluster of tea lights floating in bowls of water.

I hadn't told Vanessa about the meeting at the estate lawyer's office or that I could possibly be taking on the role of a guardian to a newborn baby. Her life as a stylist and socialite made me hesitant to disclose something like that. I didn't think she'd understand, and we didn't have that kind of relationship. Our thing was all about fun, and there wasn't anything fun about babies. At least, not to me.

As the hostess guided me to the far end of the room, Ivy came into view.

As always, her attention was on her phone, her thumbs moving along the screen at rapid speed.

"I'll call you when I'm done," I said into the phone to Vanessa. "Aight?"

She grunted. "Okay, fine."

Before I could say bye or anything else, she hung up the phone.

All I could do was shake my head.

Ivy lifted her head just in time to see me approaching.

"Thank you," I said to the hostess.

"You're very welcome." Her smile widened as she glanced at Ivy. "Should I send the waitress over now?"

"Give us a couple of minutes," Ivy answered. "Ten minutes, I think, should be enough. Thank you."

"No problem," the hostess replied. "And I hope this is okay to say, but I just love watching you two on *Free-Throw Nation* whenever you cover the Bronx Ballers games."

"Aw, thank you." Ivy peeked over at me, a small smile tugging at the corners of her lips. "I appreciate it."

"We both do," I said, getting comfortable in my seat. "Thank you."

The hostess nodded, pointing behind her with her thumb. "I'll let your waitress know to check on you guys in ten minutes."

"Sounds good." Ivy focused on me, then glanced down at her phone. "You're on time. That's new."

"Well," I said with a shrug, "a lot of things are new these days. And I'd be lying if I said it hasn't been the only thing on my mind… as seen by the way I've been playing." I dropped my head into my hands and groaned.

"I know," she replied. "It's been hard keeping it together with all this stuff happening."

I pointed at her phone. "I see it hasn't stopped your workflow, though."

"Oh, it has." She turned the phone's screen to face me, showing a maps app. "I'm testing out routes from Greene Gardens to Manhattan, trying to see how far this place is. It's a new village in the middle of practically nowhere."

"Wait." I sat up straighter in my seat. "You're looking up routes to Greene Gardens? Why?"

"That's where the house Kendra and Tyrell bought is. Remember? The one they had us visit all those months ago?"

My eyes widened. "You're considering doing this, for real, Ivy?"

She set her phone on the table and leaned back in her chair. She parted her lips to say something but closed them again.

"Look, I can't do this, man." I shook my head. "I gotta be honest with you."

Her jaw dropped. "Leo—"

"A baby is work, Ivy," I continued. "Real fucking work. They're consuming and exhausting."

"Leo—"

"Jaleel comes into practice with red eyes every day because of his two-year-old baby girl at home," I added, speaking over her. "I see how dudes change when they have babies. The game ain't played the same, they can't go out as much." I shook my head again. "I'm not looking for my life to change like that. I got my career that's just popping off. I got travel commitments." My hand was at the top of my head. "Man, all this shit is too much. The double funerals next week, having to make this decision—fuck!"

"*Shh*," Ivy shushed, checking around us. She sighed and nodded.

"I get that Mr. Grant gave us an extra day to decide, but I don't know, Ivy." I lifted my shoulders and held them there for a breath before letting them drop. "I feel like I'm about to tell this dude no, then tell his ass to find somebody else to do it, 'cause I can't."

When I finally lifted my gaze to Ivy, her eyes were slowly clouding with tears. Her lips quivered, and her chin trembled before she burst into a quiet sob.

"Damn." I scooted to the edge of my seat and reached my hand across the table to take hers. "My bad, man. Please don't cry."

She shook her head, trying her best to sniff back her tears while patting her eyes dry. "I get it," she admitted. "I'm all fucked up right now. I haven't slept since the accident. Haven't been able to think straight since the meeting with Mr. Grant."

Her wet eyes met mine, her lashes holding onto tears that hadn't yet fallen. "I don't know the first thing about babies, much less raising them. I don't know how to care for them. I literally don't think I have a maternal bone in my body, but..." She blinked, and the tears fell as she focused on me again. "They chose us."

I dropped my head and let it hang there for a few breaths.

"They chose *us*, Leo," she reminded. "They chose us. And the decision wasn't made lightly. You heard Mr. Grant."

I swallowed hard.

"They thought about it and still went to his office to not only say they wanted us to be guardians but to put that in their last will and testament. Us."

"Shit," I whispered to myself.

"Someone they made on purpose," she added. "They want to give that little person to us."

"I know." I sighed. "I know."

"Now, I don't know why the fuck Kendra would want me to raise her child if something happened to her and Tyrell," she continued. "A part of me wants to believe she just never thought it could happen and went with me thinking I'd never have to raise her baby. I don't know. Maybe she saw something in me that I don't see?"

I sat back in my seat, running my hands down my face. "Yeah, I don't know why Tyrell would even agree to something like this. I don't know if it was Kendra's idea or Tyrell's. I just... I don't know."

"Neither do I." Ivy shrugged. "But it was her last wish. Their last wish. So..." Ivy sniffed back her tears, lifting the restaurant's table napkin to dab her eyes. "If she wants me to raise this baby as my own..." She squeezed her eyes shut and inhaled deeply, stifling another cry. "Fuck it. I'm gonna do it."

I locked eyes with her across the table.

"I'm calling Mr. Grant tomorrow and telling him to move forward on the paperwork for guardianship." She forced a nod. "And if I have to do it alone, that will be fine—"

"Nah, Ivy," I said. "I can't let you do that." I shook my head. "I won't."

We stared at each other for a few beats before the weight of my words set in.

My elbows rested on the table, my head in my hand as I tried as hard as I could but failed to hold back the loud growl of frustration that echoed around us.

"*Shh,*" Ivy shushed again, her eyes darting around the restaurant. "Keep it down."

This had all been so fucking much. I felt it every damn day in my chest and my stomach, from the moment I opened my eyes after the little sleep I could manage. It had become a nightmare I couldn't wake up from. But I couldn't let Ivy do this shit alone.

She had just as much going for her as I did. I'd seen how hard she worked to get where she was in sports journalism—watched her make sacrifices, burn the midnight oil, and break through in a male-dominated field while still being unapologetically herself. She'd put in the work, and she was still willing to do this... to raise a baby.

Oh my God, we're about to raise a baby.

"I don't want you to do this alone," I said, lifting my head out of my hands. "Tyrell would kick my ass if I did."

Ivy scoffed a laugh.

We sat in silence for a few moments before Ivy spoke again. "Do you know what this reminds me of?"

"What?"

"Our first date," she replied. "Do you remember it? The one they talked us into going on and abandoned us—"

"To go hook up in the damn car," I finished for her. "*My* fucking car."

Ivy laughed, and I couldn't help but laugh too.

"I could not stand you that night," she said, shaking her head. "You were so obnoxious with your *Ivy League* this and *Ivy League* that."

"You were mad uptight," I reminded her. "At the restaurant, asking them to make the water the right amount of hot to sanitize your damn utensils."

"They kept bringing tepid ass water, which wouldn't have done shit," she argued. "Do you know how many people eat with these things on any given day?" She peeked down at her utensils and hiked a lip at it in disgust.

I snorted. "I knew then we weren't fit for each other but that you were cool enough to hang with."

She smiled. "Same."

I never stopped thinking she was beautiful, though. Even as she sat there, not her usual made-up self, with her hair in the messiest bun I'd ever seen her wear and her barest skin showing in public. Even wearing grief, the sadness evident in her face and the slump of her shoulders, Ivy was so damn gorgeous.

Too bad we were so incompatible.

"That night, they were ridiculously drunk, flaunting their fake IDs and underage-drinking bravado," Ivy recalled, her smile growing wider. "I swear she drank more that night than any other night since she and I became friends."

"I knew Tyrell before freshman year in college, and I can say he never drank that much either."

Ivy snickered. "But we worked so well together getting them back to the dorms."

I nodded. "We did."

"Couldn't stand each other the whole time, but..." She tilted her head in my direction. "We did good."

"We did great," I added.

"Then there was that time we went hiking," Ivy said, "and Kendra sprained her ankle. You and I figured out how to administer first aid, and then you went searching and found park rangers to help out."

I pointed at her. "That shit was crazy, but we came through, for real."

"And we do a great job on the air too," she added. "Whenever I'm interviewing you?"

I nodded. "The fans love us. Love it even more when we annoy each other."

"And we did the damn thing with the baby shower," she said, pointing at me. "Because what the hell did we know about throwing a baby shower?"

"Not a damn thing," I replied with a chuckle. "And that shit was an event to remember."

"She absolutely loved it." Ivy's smile widened. "She thought we did so good."

"Tyrell, too."

"So, you know... maybe..." She folded her bottom lip into her mouth. "Maybe we could do this too."

"It's a baby, though, Ivy," I said, my eyes locking on hers. "A real baby that breathes, cries, shits, and does all the other shit that makes me thank God every day that I never got a woman pregnant and pray that I *never* will."

Ivy hollered a laugh. "I know." Her smile softened as she met my gaze with her beautiful brown eyes. "I just feel like doing this, somehow, is going to make me feel better about all this."

I blinked in response.

"Taking care of this baby is going to make me feel like I don't have a hole in my heart where Kendra used to be, you know?"

This whole thing was scaring the shit out of me. As I sat there, visualizing what this would look like, I couldn't see myself in the role of caring for someone so small and vulnerable.

I wasn't the most responsible person—I'd never admit that, but it was true. I liked to party, travel on a whim, and have casual sex with women in random ass places for the thrill. I was not father material in the least.

But I couldn't let Ivy do this alone.

Now her? She would be great at this. She didn't think so, but that was an Ivy thing—worrying about everything because she was a perfectionist to the bone. She would excel at this, no question about it. And I would simply let her lead.

The least I could do was support her and help out wherever I could—which I knew wouldn't be all that much.

"Aight, look," I said, moving to the edge of my seat. "We both know I'm about to suck at this shit. Let's just keep it real."

"Leo—"

"But I want to do this with you because I know you *won't* suck at it."

She tilted her head to one side.

"You're smart," I started. "A fucking genius. The way your mind works fast, it amazes me sometimes—shit, a lot of the time."

She blushed, dropping her head to hide it.

"So I'm confident we'll be fine."

"We?" she asked. "Does that mean you'll do it with me?"

I smirked. "We still talking about the baby, right?"

She kissed her teeth. "Really? Yuck!"

I tossed my head back, laughing, and she giggled.

Leveling my gaze, I said, "Yeah, let's do this guardianship thing. We'll figure it out."

She closed her eyes and exhaled a deep breath, pressing her prayer hands to her lips. "Okay."

We spent the rest of the time exchanging ideas and hopes about what this new journey would entail. During the quiet moments as we ate dinner, my mind raced with all the things I would need to do.

Was I giving up my loft?

How far was Greene Gardens from the city?

Were there other people living there already, or would we be the only ones moving into the village?

"He doesn't have a name," Ivy said, pulling me out of my thoughts.

"What?"

"Their baby." Ivy lifted her napkin to pat her lips clean. "I just remembered that he doesn't have a name. When I asked Kendra what they came up with, she said we'd have to find out when he's born and they tell us, but..."

I squeezed my eyes closed and dropped my head back between my shoulders.

"I don't want to name him just anything—"

"We'll ask Kendra and Tyrell's parents," I said with a nod. "We'll ask their parents if either of them knows. Kendra and Tyrell had to at least have told their parents, right?"

"Right." Ivy nodded, her expression softening. "Yeah, they had to have."

"For now, though," I started, "let's just take it one step at a time."

Ivy grinned. "Look at you being the voice of reason."

I shrugged a shoulder. "Just tryna get my head right here."

She snickered.

I lifted my glass of scotch and held it in the air. Ivy, needing no instruction, lifted her glass of red wine and tapped her glass gently against mine.

"To Kendra and Tyrell," I said as our glasses clinked.

"And to us," Ivy added, bringing the rim of her glass to her lips.

"Yeah," I whispered to myself. "To us."

ivy

I STOOD at the floor-to-ceiling window, staring out at the vast land in front of me. My eyes scanned the expansive backyard, where the growing landscape of Greene Gardens offered a faded green backdrop. We were days away from the start of winter, and the temperature mirrored that—likely contributing to the muted green color spread out before me. I imagined it would look much better when spring rolled around. At the moment, it looked a bit dull, but I could see its potential.

"That was the last box," Leo said behind me, pulling my attention away from the window.

I nodded in acknowledgment, turning to face him, my arms still tightly folded across my chest.

Leo entered the house without needing to duck his head. He and Tyrell were close to the same height, so I was sure the high ceilings and tall doorjambs were built with intention, keeping Tyrell and his friends in mind.

Leo and I were really doing it. We'd done it. Signed the guardianship papers Mr. Grant had forwarded to the courts, signed the new deed on Kendra and Tyrell's property in Greene Gardens, and uprooted our lives to move out to the middle of nowhere.

A sharp cry echoed from upstairs. Leo and I both turned toward the sound before refocusing on each other.

"I got him," Marta, the baby nurse, said, taking quick steps from the back of the house toward the stairs. "This is very good. Very, very good," she added. "He got up the same time yesterday."

I turned to Leo. "He got up the same time yesterday... whatever that means."

He scoffed a laugh, turning away to press his hands to the top of his head.

So much had happened since we agreed to take on the responsibility of being guardians to Kendra and Tyrell's son.

The very next day, I was on the internet, trying to find all I could about taking care of babies—writing down a list of books I decided I would listen to in audio instead of read to save time. There were so many, though. Too many to choose from. By the time I got to the fifth recommendation, I felt like I was having a panic attack.

Thankfully, I had the sense to call Kendra's mother and ask her what she recommended I read. She chuckled at the thought, telling me she needed the laugh.

"Ivy, baby, there isn't a book in the world that's going to prepare you for this."

It wasn't what I wanted to hear, and it didn't help my anxiety one bit. She must've sensed that because she told me if I ran into any trouble, she and her husband, Kendra's father Walt, would be there to guide Leo and me. She also suggested hiring a baby nurse, explaining that a coworker had done that for her second child to get some relief at night.

My next few phone calls were to agencies, searching for a qualified baby nurse. I found one who met the standards I'd set—with Leo's fairly limited but fair input.

Marta Ramirez was the first person to stay in Kendra and Tyrell's house. She accompanied us to the hospital to pick up the baby and bring him to the Greene Gardens property.

The first time I laid eyes on him, I couldn't stop staring. He looked so much like Kendra—his eyes, his lips. I wasn't even sure Tyrell had been in the room the night he was made. I was also too scared to touch him. He was so tiny and fragile-looking. Since we brought him home two days ago, I hadn't touched him once—just watched him as he slept.

Leo sighed, turning to face me again. "How long is Marta staying with us again?"

"One month," I answered. "She said starting tomorrow, we'll have sessions with her to learn the basics—like how to pick him up, hold him, and soothe him when he's upset."

Leo inhaled deeply, letting it out through pursed lips. "I got a game in like three days," he revealed. "An away game, so..."

I nodded. "I remember."

Leo gestured at me. "How about you? When are you heading back to work?"

"In two weeks," I said, pointing toward the stairs. "Around the time Marta says we'll be able to handle at least the daily responsibilities while she takes care of nights until her month with us is up. Then we'll need to hire a nanny... but." I held up a hand. "One step at a time, right?"

Leo bobbed his head up and down. "Yeah."

My eyes drifted from Leo to scan the surrounding space. Kendra and Tyrell's home, which was now Leo's and mine, was stunning. It was clear they'd intended for it to be their forever family home. The ground floor boasted a large living room that flowed into a dining area and a state-of-the-art kitchen, equipped with everything you could imagine. There was also an office and floor-to-ceiling windows that opened to the biggest backyard I'd ever seen in New York State.

Our bedrooms were upstairs. Leo had insisted I take the master bedroom with the en suite, and I'd accepted quickly before he could change his mind. From the kitchen to the attic, the home had a sleek, contemporary design with an insanely spacious layout.

Kendra had invited me more times than I could count to check out their build in Greene Gardens, but I was stuck on staying in the city. She kept raving about the land they'd bought through the village's custom home lot program, which lets buyers design their own places instead of buying one of those prefab models. Despite all her enthusiasm, I just wasn't buying into the idea of moving there. Everyone was talking about moving out of New York City, but I hadn't wanted to hear it. I would've missed out if I'd never agreed to come here when she invited me. Even still under construction, the village was beautiful, with clear potential.

"Okay," Marta said as she descended the stairs. "He's back asleep."

"He sleeps a lot, huh?" Leo asked. "That's great."

Marta giggled. "They sleep a lot the first couple of weeks. They're getting acclimated to being out of the womb."

"So..." I turned to face her. "That's not, like... a forever thing?"

Marta laughed, covering her mouth as she glanced toward the stairs. "No, mami. It is not forever."

I looked to Leo.

"You two settle in," Marta said. "Rest up. Tomorrow, we'll start the first session in the morning."

She left the area, heading toward the ground-floor office we'd turned into her temporary bedroom.

Tyrell's mother had said something similar—when she wasn't bursting into tears staring at a picture of her grandson. She'd taken the loss of her son very hard, understandably, but she was gracious enough to offer to watch the baby if Leo and I ever needed a break. Kendra's parents had offered as well, as had Leo's mother and mine.

"Have you started unpacking?" I asked Leo.

"Nah, you?"

"Of course." I nodded.

"Why am I not surprised?" He smirked.

"I mean, I still have some boxes of shoes and stuff, but yeah, most of my things are set. I don't like to wait."

"Hmph."

I turned toward the stairs. "Come on, I can help you unpack."

"Uh…" Leo caught me by the wrist.

I glanced down at his grip, then up at his eyes.

"That's aight." He forced a smile, releasing my wrist. "I'll take care of it."

I tilted my head to one side. "Leo, it's no big deal. We'll just handle the basics—"

"I said, I'm cool."

I stared at him for a moment, and he stared back.

"You didn't bring no drugs in here, right?"

His brows furrowed. "What?"

"Because I don't want that here." I folded my arms over my chest. "I've never been around babies, but I'm pretty sure drugs and babies don't go."

He kissed his teeth. "I didn't bring drugs in here, Ivy. Come on, man."

I held my stare for another beat before shaking my head and looking away.

"I just…" Leo started, running his hands down his face. "I want to take my time. I get it—we're here now, cool. But I'm not like you."

He exhaled and let his attention wander around the space. His eyes landed on the walls, where contemporary art pieces and photographs of landscapes already decorated the house.

"It takes a little time for me to get adjusted to shit," he admitted. "I haven't even put my loft up for sale yet. And now I'm living in a house out here in a village that's still under construction. Life is coming at me too damn fast."

"Tell me about it," I mumbled. "We'll be fine, though."

His gaze shifted back to me.

"Everything is crazy, and we don't quite know what to expect," I said, lifting my shoulders in a shrug before letting them drop. "But… we'll be fine."

"Shit." He released a nervous chuckle. "I sure hope so because when that baby cried just now, my heart jumped and hasn't landed back in my chest yet."

"Right?!" I giggled. "Like, I literally felt my heart hit the ceiling, and it's still up there."

We both laughed before taking deep breaths at the same time.

"We're doing the right thing," I said, meeting his eyes again. "Everything we're doing... we're making the right decision."

He smirked. "I'm praying that's true, Ivy League."

I pointed at him, and he threw his hands up in surrender, laughing.

I sighed and let my eyes wander up the stairs that led to the bedrooms. A thought crossed my mind.

"He still doesn't have a name," I reminded, looking back at Leo.

"I know."

After checking with both Kendra's parents and Tyrell's mother, we learned that Kendra and Tyrell hadn't shared their potential baby names with them like we'd hoped. So Leo and I were completely in the dark about where to start. The hospital staff were understanding, though, offering to file the birth certificate with the placeholder name *'Baby Boy Love'* until we decided on a permanent one.

I had no idea where to even start. Neither Kendra nor Tyrell's parents knew what they'd planned to name their son. Hell, Kendra and Tyrell didn't even know the baby's gender—they'd kept telling Leo and me that we'd find out after the baby was born.

"I don't want to just choose a name," I said, shaking my head. "Names are important. They shape personalities."

"We could name him after Tyrell," Leo suggested with a shrug. "Like, Tyrell Love, Jr."

"They didn't want that. I at least know that much," I said. "When I asked if they'd name the baby after Tyrell if it was a boy, Tyrell was quick to say no. He hated his name."

Leo snorted. "He really did."

That made me giggle too. I tucked my lips into my mouth, thinking. "We have to call him something."

"Baby sounds good to me," Leo said with a grin.

"Baby?"

He laughed. "Yeah. Simple. To the point, until we think of something else."

I lifted my gaze to the ceiling, scanning it as if it had answers... and, in a way, it kind of did.

"How about *Baby Love*?"

Leo arched a brow. "Baby Love?"

"Yeah." I nodded. "Baby, like you suggested, and Love for Kendra and Tyrell's last name—which is his last name too. Baby Love."

Leo's eyes moved around the room before he nodded. "Aight, sure. Baby Love."

I smiled. Something about agreeing on something together made me feel a little better about the situation. "Okay, cool. We'll keep researching and trying out names in the meantime."

"And in *my* meantime..." Leo stretched his arms high and yawned for effect. "I'm gonna get some sleep while I still can."

"I'm gonna see what else I can set up down here," I said, looking around the space.

"Marta said rest up, Ivy League." He smirked. "I think you should take her advice."

"Would you stop calling me that!"

He chuckled as he headed toward the stairs. "It's gonna be really interesting living with you in this big-ass house, roomie."

"*Mm-hmm.*" I shook my head while grinning. "Hopefully, I don't kill you in the process."

SIX

1 MONTH LATER...

"OH MY GOD," I groaned, my eyes falling on everything that shouldn't be where it was. "Is he *fucking* kidding me right now?!"

I wanted to scream at the top of my lungs. The scream was right there, boiling in my throat, waiting to erupt—but the hour stopped me.

It was barely daybreak. Through the floor-to-ceiling windows, I could see the sun hadn't risen yet, as usual for the time I got up.

My shoulders sagged as my eyes landed on the cluttered living room—not how I'd left it when I dragged myself off to bed the night before.

I'd made a point to come downstairs and clear the papers and water bottles left by both me and Leo. He'd had training all day yesterday, and I'd been working from home, leaving the living area in a state of chaos. Even though the nanny we'd hired helped a lot during the day, there were still plenty of hours left for us to make a mess. But keeping the house tidy? That was all on me.

I sighed as I walked into the living room, picking up sneakers, socks, granola bar wrappers, and water bottles—most of which still had water in them.

"I'm gonna kill him," I muttered, tossing his sneakers toward the shoe rack.

I'd gotten that shoe rack for him. Leo. Because this wasn't the first time he'd left things all over the place.

Every night when he came home, he peeled off his clothes—shirt, joggers, whatever—and let them fall wherever. And he never came back to pick them up.

He was driving me crazy.

The slight creak of the stairs caught my attention over my shoulder as I hunched forward to pick up yet another item of clothing.

"What's up, Ivy League?" Leo greeted, jogging down the remainder of the stairs.

"*Shh*," I shushed, standing upright and turning to face him. "He's still sleeping, and I'd like for him to stay asleep until Karina gets here."

Karina was Baby Love's nanny, and she was a godsend. Our baby nurse, Marta, had taught us everything we needed to know in what felt like a crash course. Days of lessons on everything from holding the baby to changing, bathing, burping, and soothing him. It was a lot, even just thinking back on it, but it helped so much.

"Aight, my bad." He chuckled.

Even that irritated me.

I was running on maybe three or four hours of sleep. Between driving to the city every other day and then coming back here to edit videos for upload, I wasn't sleeping. With no baby nurse to handle Baby Love at night, Leo and I were on our own. Well, mostly me. Unlike Leo, I wasn't out in Manhattan at a club, making appearances or partying like I didn't have new responsibilities in a new home.

"You look rested," I commented, resuming my task of picking up yesterday's leftovers.

"I'm feeling good, feeling great," he replied, rolling his head from side to side. "Yo, have you seen my wallet?"

I rolled my eyes and turned back to picking up the mess. "Now, why would I know where your wallet is, Leo?"

"Damn," he said with a snicker. "Why so cranky?"

I whipped my head in his direction, then turned to face him fully. "Maybe because for yet another morning, I'm down here cleaning up your shit that you could have *easily* put away when you got back home?"

He threw his hands up. "I said my bad."

"*My bad* doesn't do shit for me, Leo." I shrugged. "It just doesn't."

"Aight, fine." He grunted. "I'll look for my own wallet then, damn."

I stared at him for a moment, seriously contemplating chucking the bottles and snack wrappers at him. Instead, I inhaled a deep breath, closing my eyes to force myself to calm down.

I'd never lived with a man before—for this reason exactly. Kendra had been so excited to move in with Tyrell back in college, and I'd never understood why. Living with someone had never been something I wanted.

Even in college, I could barely stand my roommates because they were so messy.

Was it too much to ask to put things away when done? To throw out wrappers after finishing whatever was inside?

"Look," I said to him. "We're both busy. And I get it—we're both adjusting to living here and taking care of a baby neither one of us expected to have to take care of. But, Leo, *please*." I sighed. "Do your fucking part."

He turned to face me, folding his arms over his broad chest.

"I shouldn't be starting my day like this." I gestured around the room. "Your shit is everywhere except where it's supposed to be. The least you can do is put it away when you get home."

"I was tired," he reasoned. "When I got back, I just wanted everything off me so I could get into bed."

"Same," I shot back. "I feel the same way when I get home. I just wanted to come down here, get some coffee before the baby gets up, and I have to take care of him until the nanny shows up. But here I am, wasting my time cleaning up your shit."

"Aight, oh-fucking-kay," he said. "I'll do my best to do better."

I rolled my eyes, closing them briefly.

"But for real, Ivy, I'm not about to make promises I'm not sure I can keep," he added. "I'm not as uptight as you, so, you know…"

I jerked my head back.

"I just let it hang a lot of the time." He pressed a hand to his chest. "For me, it ain't really that big of a deal. Just clean it up, and I'll try to be mindful next time."

"This conversation is not making me feel any better," I said flatly. "Just so you know."

He lifted his arms, letting them drop. Then he patted his pocket and pulled out his wallet.

"Ha!" He laughed a little too hard. "I had it the whole time."

Just then, Baby Love's sharp cry pierced the air from his nursery upstairs.

I closed my eyes and collapsed my head back.

"Whew," Leo said, grinning. "That's my cue."

He walked up to me, bent slightly, and pressed his lips to my cheek. Then he blew air against my skin, making my face rattle.

I punched his arm, and he laughed even louder.

"Sleep with one eye open tonight, Leo," I threatened. "I swear I hate you."

"Love you too," he replied with a chuckle. "See you later. Don't worry about food—I'll bring dinner back for you."

I shook my head, dropping the clutter in my hands onto the couch before heading toward the stairs.

All the nervousness I'd had about handling the baby had subsided after the days I spent learning under our baby nurse, Marta. I paid special attention to the small details she shared about caring for him, and it seemed to have paid off.

His cries grew louder the moment I opened the door but began to settle as I approached his bassinet.

"Good morning," I said the moment our eyes met. I couldn't help but smile at the sight of him. He looked so much like Kendra—especially those eyes. "Why are you crying so loudly and so early in the morning? I haven't even had my coffee yet."

As soon as I lifted him and laid him against my chest, the crying stopped completely.

I walked over to the section of his room that housed his bottles, the bottle warmer, a few framed photos, and the small fridge Marta recommended we keep in the nursery for easy access to his formula. One of those framed photos was of Kendra and Tyrell on their wedding day. Leo and I kept it on the baby's dresser as our way of helping Baby Love remember his roots, despite his parents not being around.

Our nanny had left a bottle in the warmer before ending her shift the night before, so it was perfectly ready for Baby Love's morning feeding.

When it came to schedules, Baby Love was consistent. That's where he and I connected. He did everything according to schedule, including feeding, and I loved the predictability. It was one of the few things to love in this situation.

I took a seat in the rocking chair and laid him in position to start feeding. As always, he was eager, latching onto the bottle's nipple and suckling his milk right away.

"How about Bradley?" I whispered, my eyes locked on his. "Anthony?"

We were still trying out names. It was a miracle Leo and I had been allowed to go this long without settling on Baby Love's first name. I was the only one making suggestions, though.

"Corey?" I whispered next before shaking my head. "I dated a Corey and hated that ninja, so let's not do that one."

I smiled down at Baby Love, watching his eyes slowly close as he drifted back to sleep. Holding him felt so right—warm, cuddly, and trusting. I had worried he might sense my inexperience the moment

I first held him, but he took to me better than I had hoped. That was what I loved most of all.

Both the baby nurse and the nanny had said that all this sleeping would stop soon, and honestly, I wasn't looking forward to it. If I could barely handle life while Baby Love was still an infant, what was I going to do when he started sleeping less?

"Hopefully, your Uncle Leo will grow the hell up before you start sleeping less," I mumbled. "Because I sure could use the help."

SEVEN

I TURNED my head to peer through the glass windows of the house. The lights were on, which meant Ivy was up—not surprising.

The woman didn't sleep. I knew she worked hard, but damn, I hardly ever saw her resting. Especially not after we accepted guardianship of Baby Love.

I scoffed a laugh, leaning my head back against the headrest. We still hadn't decided on a name. Every day, every time Ivy laid eyes on that baby, she was trying out names like she tried on designer heels at a boutique.

It was funny—and kind of cute.

I sat in my car, my eyes volleying between the house our friends left us and the empty streets of the neighborhood we now called home.

When Tyrell told me about the land and house he bought in a village outside New York City, I thought he was crazy.

"Couldn't be me," I said to him as I shook my head for emphasis. "The house, the wife, and the baby? Man." I blew air out my mouth. "Miss me with all that bullshit. Please."

"You're just out here, 30 years old, big as all hell, and scared of love," Tyrell chuckled beside me. "How sad."

"You damn right I'm scared." I leaned forward in my seat to snatch up a shot of Jack. "So scared, my ass needs to take a drink to calm my nerves that've been rattled just at the thought. Fuck that."

Tyrell and I were in the VIP section in the club he had accompanied me out to in Queens for a special appearance I had. It was rare for Tyrell to join me for something like this. Since he and his wife, Kendra, got married, Tyrell didn't make it out as much. We used to hit up a concert at least once a year, 90s themed, and then the club after, but I was pretty sure that next year, hitting up the concert with him, his wife, and her best friend Ivy and then the club, wasn't going to happen with this new baby on the way.

But that night, he insisted we chill since we hadn't seen much of each other since he and his wife announced their pregnancy earlier in the year. The basketball season had just started for me, and I was either training for games or away playing in another state.

"You know," I started, "you should probably scoot your ass over a little on this couch so I don't catch what you got."

Tyrell tossed his head back in a laugh.

"I'm serious, Rell, please." I shoved him away playfully. "Move over that way."

Tyrell shoved me back, which made me laugh.

Club music reverberated off the walls around us. It was loud as hell in the club, but for me, this was my natural habitat. I loved everything about the nightlife.

"The wife already gives me life, and this baby is about to do the same," Tyrell started. *"And the house?" He smiled big like a man who just won the lottery. "The house already is feeling like a home I can't wait to get into permanently."*

It had only been a month, and it still didn't feel like home... or anything like what Tyrell was looking forward to experiencing.

For one, Greene Gardens was *quiet*. Sure, it was a new development, a new town, with very few residents calling it home. But it was more than that—it was too quiet. No honking horns, no kids playing on the newly paved sidewalks. No smells of nicotine or street meat sizzling on grills that probably hadn't been cleaned in months.

It wasn't New York City. It wasn't home to me.

Sometimes it felt like I was driving through a movie lot after hours—that's how quiet and empty it was.

I did this every night I came back—sat in the car long after I arrived.

Most nights, I wasn't even coming home from a game or practice. Any reason to leave the house, I took it. Club appearances. Grabbing something from my loft in the city. Hell, even just driving to Manhattan to smell smog or catch a whiff of a dirty tailpipe. Any excuse to escape Greene Gardens and delay the reminder that my life had flipped upside down, I took it.

Like now.

The only thing that eventually got me out of my car was knowing Ivy was inside. She'd given up just as much as I had—and then some. She was in there right now, taking care of a baby she never planned to have. I was sure she missed the city as much as I did, but she didn't get the same opportunities to escape it.

That thought—and my mother's voice in my head—finally got me moving.

"You better not leave Ivy to do everything, Leo," my mother, Cheryl, had told me when I showed up unannounced at her place.

It was late—almost ten—and instead of being happy to see me, she wasn't even letting me in.

"It's just as much of a shock and adjustment for her as it is for you," she said, standing in the doorway.

"Are you gonna let me in, Ma?"

"No." She shook her head, leaning against the doorframe. "Because if you're here, that means Ivy's home with that baby—alone. And I'm not aiding and abetting."

I chuckled, shifting my stance on her doorstep. "Excuse me?"

"Go home, Leo," she said with a knowing smile. "Go be the man I raised you to be."

I closed my eyes now and inhaled deeply. When was this going to feel like home? When would it click for me to be as hands-on as Ivy? When did it click for her?

My gaze fell to the bags of takeout sitting on the passenger seat.

At the very least, I could bring home dinner.

Since moving here with the baby, I'd taken on the task of getting food from the city—a convenient excuse to escape to Manhattan. Ivy wasn't much of a cook, and while my mother made it a priority for me to learn how to cook growing up under her roof, I simply didn't feel like cooking as an adult. Between caring for the baby and everything else, we barely had time to figure out a proper meal routine. We were still sorting through profiles for housekeepers and possibly a cook.

It was a lot.

I sighed, grabbed the plastic handles of the takeout bags, and pushed open the door to step out.

The night was cold. We'd had our first snowfall recently, and people I knew who lived in Upstate New York said it could've been worse. They told me I should be grateful for how mild this first winter in Greene Gardens was.

When I stepped into the house, the scent of lemon cleaner hit me.

Everything was in its place—nothing on the floors or surfaces within view.

I snickered as I unlaced my sneakers. I was seconds away from kicking them off when I remembered my promise to Ivy.

I set the takeout bags on the small table by the front door, then removed my sneakers and placed them neatly on the shoe rack she had bullied me into using.

Cleanliness wasn't my thing. It just wasn't.

My mom had always cleaned up after me without complaint. In college, my roommate was just as messy as me, so we only cleaned when we had company—which was often, but it didn't make us any less messy. Once I got into the league and started making money, I hired someone to handle it. And they didn't complain either—because I paid them well.

Seeing Ivy get all upset over me leaving my stuff wherever it fell was both comical and sobering.

Speaking of which, I didn't see or hear her or the baby anywhere on the ground floor.

I glanced at my watch, noting it was about the time Ivy would usually be in the office we'd set up after the baby nurse left—or maybe in the kitchen.

Like I said, she barely slept, so the last place I expected her to be was in bed.

Still, I wanted to make sure everything was good before I sat down to eat.

Kendra and Tyrell had done a great job getting this property together before... well, before everything happened. Ivy and I had added our own touches since moving in—our way of trying to make it feel like our own.

I was still waiting for it to actually feel that way.

On the second floor, where all three bedrooms were, only one room had its light on: Baby Love's nursery.

I hadn't spent much time with the baby, to be honest. Between games in the city and away, and my own need to escape this new reality, I wasn't home much. And when I was, I found it hard to be around him.

Every time I looked at him, my heart hurt.

It wasn't just the weight of being responsible for a life when I could barely keep myself together. It was the way he reminded me so much of what I'd lost.

My best friend, Tyrell.

Ivy always said Baby Love looked like Kendra—and he did. But to me, his mannerisms were all Tyrell. Even as a baby, he was alert like his dad. He smiled like his dad too. His essence, his presence—it was all Tyrell.

And every time I looked into that baby's eyes, it felt like hearing the news for the first time all over again.

When would *that* get better?

Because shit—it had been an entire month.

I approached the nursery's door, which was slightly ajar. The plan was to poke my head in just long enough to let Ivy know I was home. It was quiet. No crying or even cooing from Baby Love, and I didn't want to risk waking him.

That was another thing I struggled with—being quiet enough not to disturb him. Somehow, everything I did seemed to make him stir. Walking around the house. Greeting Ivy in the mornings. Hell, even *breathing*.

Ivy, on the other hand, had become a ninja. She could leave a room without making a sound after putting him back to sleep, and even make her coffee quietly in the mornings. She'd adapted. I hadn't.

And that was just another reason I found myself out of the house as much as possible.

When I leaned in and peered through the door, I glimpsed the peaceful woodland mural on the accent wall. Raising my hand, I prepared to get Ivy's attention—but instead, I froze.

Ivy stood in the middle of the nursery, cradling Baby Love in her arms. Her long hair, which she usually wore in a neat, slick bun, was down and flowing.

In all the years I'd known her, I'd only seen her hair down twice —once at Kendra and Tyrell's wedding, when Kendra had bullied her into wearing it loose, and now.

I always knew her hair was long from the volume of her buns, but I didn't know it was *this* long now. The ends were just inches above her waist, making her figure stand out more—her curves, her ass, her legs.

She wore a patterned designer robe I hadn't seen before, one that showed off her full legs and her bare feet. When she turned her head slightly, glancing over her shoulder, my jaw nearly dropped.

Now, hear me out.

Back when Kendra and Tyrell first started dating in college, Kendra had introduced me to Ivy. She'd sworn up and down I would fall for her best friend. And I'd thought Ivy was beautiful, no question.

She had that 90s Jet Beauty of the Week kind of appeal. Ivy resembled the late singer Aaliyah. Light brown complexion, communicative eyes, and picture-perfect smile and all. So, yeah—I knew she wasn't some ogre. But we'd friend-zoned each other so fast it was like a reflex.

We were *too* different.

She was uptight, particular, and rigid. Everything I did during our one and only date was an issue. My jokes? She turned her nose up at them. My charm? Didn't work. The small sliver of cleavage peeking out from her blouse? She'd covered it the second I noticed it. It was like going on a date with one of my mother's friends.

Beautiful, yes—but not my type.

Now, though? Seeing her standing there in that robe, her face completely bare—no lashes, no makeup, no lip gloss, just her naturally pink lips and glowing skin—I was rethinking all of it.

"Gahdamn," I muttered before clearing my throat. "I mean, what's up?"

She lifted a finger to her lips, signaling for me to keep quiet.

She repositioned Baby Love, laying him against her shoulder and gently patting his bottom to soothe him.

I pushed the door open slightly, taking in the scene as she rocked him for a moment longer. Then she leaned over the bassinet, carefully placing him inside.

My eyes followed the curve of her waist to her round ass, then down to her legs—where they stayed. Legs were my thing. Always had been. And Ivy? She had some *sexy* legs.

How had I not noticed before?

I must've gotten lost in my stare because I didn't realize Ivy had closed the distance between us until she pressed a finger to my forehead, forcing my gaze back up to her face.

"What the fuck are you looking at?" she whispered, her brows raised in mock annoyance.

I let out a scoffing laugh as she pushed me back and out of the nursery.

She turned to close the door, slowly and carefully, so the lock wouldn't click.

My eyes wandered again, tracing the strands of her hair to her ass, and then settling back on her legs.

"Did you just get in?" she asked, flicking on the hallway light and turning to face me.

"Yeah," I said, forcing myself to focus on her face. Not that it helped. Under the light, her features looked even softer.

She stared at me for a moment before asking, "What?"

"Huh?"

"Why are you staring at me like that?" she asked, her voice low. "What's going on with you?"

My gaze drifted off again before she snapped her fingers in front of my face, pulling me back.

When I refocused, I saw the furrow in her brows and the faint smirk tugging at her lips.

"Are you okay?"

"Yeah," I said, a small smile forming. "You just... you look nice."

Her brows knitted further in confusion.

"Your hair," I said, reaching out to take a strand between my fingers. "And this whole look—dressed down. I've never seen you this dressed down before. And so... relaxed."

She giggled softly. "What are you talking about, LV? I look a mess. Please."

That made me smile wider. "LV. Feels like it's been forever since you've called me that."

She dropped her gaze to her feet, then glanced toward her bedroom. "I'm going to put something on."

I wish she wouldn't.

"You're good," I insisted. "I brought food. We should head down and eat."

She scanned my face for a moment, a smirk still tugging at her lips.

I nodded toward the stairs. "Come on. I got your favorite, too."

She studied me for another beat before nodding. "Okay, cool."

I gestured for her to go first. "Ladies first."

She laughed quietly, obliging as she headed downstairs.

Little did she know, I didn't insist she go in front of me just to be polite. I just needed another look.

How had I not realized how fine she was?

ivy

"I STINK," I said aloud, lowering my gaze to Baby Love. "Thanks to you."

He opened his little mouth and let out a yawn, which made me smile.

I never really understood people's fascination with babies. Sure, they were cute, but beyond that, they didn't seem to offer much besides their presence.

But in Baby Love's case, that presence was enough.

Before all this, I would have never decided to have a baby of my own. But after spending the last month and a half with him, I started to understand the hype. I got why people chose to have them on purpose.

Everything about him made me *oooh* and *awww*. The way he'd started trying to lift his head whenever I walked into his nursery in the mornings. The way he yawned—his little mouth opening as wide as it could, but still looking so small.

The only thing I wasn't a fan of? His spit-up. He didn't do it often, but when he did, it always managed to get on me. The longer it mixed with my skin or soaked into my clothes, the sourer the smell became.

And today, he'd gotten me good.

"I need a shower," I said, cradling him in my arms as I stood from the rocking chair.

It had been two weeks since I'd been to *Free-Throw Nation's* office. Over a month since I'd covered an on-court game. My life had been turned upside down. Tomorrow, I had a meeting with my producer to discuss my future there—a future that, from where I stood, looked bleak.

I sighed, walking to the nursery door and pulling it open.

My goals before becoming one-half of Baby Love's guardianship had been crystal clear: move up at *Free-Throw Nation* and earn a seat at the anchor desk. But at this rate? The only seat I'd be getting would be on the sidelines at Baby Love's future youth basketball games, surrounded by other moms and caregivers.

Honestly, I felt like I was the only one giving up so much.

Leo hadn't changed a single thing since we became guardians. The only thing different about his life was his zip code. Every chance he got, he was in the city—partying, making club appearances, living his best single life.

He hadn't even suggested a name for the baby. We were still calling him Baby Love.

On nights like this, I usually toughed it out on my own. Leo was either playing a game in the city, attending sponsorship events, or partying. Oddly enough, he was home tonight.

And that was a blessing, because I desperately needed a shower.

"Geoffrey?" I asked, peeking down at Baby Love. "Nah, you don't look like a Geoffrey. Maybe Morgan?"

His eyes locked on mine, and a little smile tugged at his lips.

"You like that one?" I asked. "Morgan? Sounds kind of girly to me. I don't know."

Without thinking, I found myself in front of Leo's door. I needed a shower—badly—and instead of knocking, I turned the knob and walked right in.

I hardly ever went into Leo's room. Since he was rarely home, there was never a reason to.

The door opened easily, and there he was, sitting at his desk with his back to me. His head bobbed up and down, oversized headphones covering his ears. Muffled music blasted at full volume.

I passed his massive flat-screen TV and entertainment center, breezing by the sports memorabilia and awards he'd brought from his loft in the city. His king-sized bed was unmade—not surprising—and I didn't even bother commenting on it.

As I got closer, I noticed the piles and piles of LEGO bricks scattered across his desk.

"What in the world?" I asked, a smile tugging at my lips.

Leo's head snapped up. He jumped in his chair, visibly torn between lowering his headphones or hiding the LEGO bricks.

My jaw dropped as my smile widened. "Oh my God! Is your grown ass playing with Legos?"

"Yo!" he said, jumping to his feet and yanking the headphones off. "Do you not know how to knock?"

I couldn't take my eyes off what he was building.

It wasn't finished yet, but the vision was clear.

"Is this a LEGO Mona Lisa?" I made a shrugging motion with the sides of my mouth. "Dope."

Leo glanced down at Baby Love in my arms, then sighed as he looked at the half-built creation. He ran a hand down his face.

"First of all," he started, "I'm not *playing* with Legos. I'm *building*. Like the builders or whoever they are building these houses in this village."

I snorted.

"Second of all, what are you doing in here?"

"I need a shower," I said, lifting Baby Love higher in my arms. "He didn't fall asleep like he usually does, and I can't take smelling like sour milk anymore. I just can't. I need you to watch him."

Leo's eyes widened. "What?"

"I need you to watch him," I repeated, moving closer and holding the baby out to him. "He's so close to falling asleep. He yawned twice —like Marta said babies do right before they knock out. But I can't wait any longer. I keep smelling myself, and I'm gagging."

"I... I don't know, Ivy." Leo scratched the back of his head. "I don't want to break him."

My brows furrowed. "Huh?"

"I'm not good at holding him."

"Because you don't hold him enough. *Duh.*" I sighed. "You're always out in the city, playing games or making club appearances. I wasn't good at holding him at first either. The only way I got better was with practice. Like most things."

"Ivy—"

"You gotta start somewhere. Here." I gestured to the chair he'd been sitting in. "Sit."

"Ivy—"

"*Sit,*" I said, lowering my voice when Baby Love stirred.

Leo sighed, inhaling a deep breath and exhaling slowly before finally doing as I said.

"You're a righty, right?" I asked.

"Yeah," he mumbled.

"Okay," I said, stepping closer. "You want to keep your left arm a little higher so you can cradle him, and use your right hand for extra support."

"Aight," Leo muttered.

I tried to fight back my smile but found it impossible. I'd never seen Leo like this before. He was always making a joke, the life of the party, or the cool and collected LV on the court, even during the most intense games. Seeing him this nervous—over something as simple as holding a tiny human—was adorable.

As soon as I laid Baby Love in Leo's arms, Leo inhaled deeply and held his breath.

I fought back a laugh. "Will you breathe, please?"

Baby Love stirred slightly, letting out one of his usual baby sounds.

"He aight?" Leo asked, his eyes locked on the baby. "He sounds uncomfortable. Like I'm hurting him."

"He's just getting comfortable," I assured him. "Relax and get comfortable, too."

Leo adjusted himself in the chair, leaning back a little, relaxing his arms.

The sight before me was... breathtaking.

Leo was the quintessential handsome athlete: strong arms, broad shoulders, a chiseled chest. But his face? Perfect facial symmetry. That's what made him an undeniable heartthrob. And yet, despite all that, I'd never seen him look as good as he did right now, holding Baby Love.

"There you go," I said softly, unable to stop staring. "You got it."

Leo's eyes stayed on Baby Love. A small smile crept onto his lips as he watched the baby. "He smells good."

"So good." I giggled. "Meanwhile, I'm the one who smells like spit-up."

Leo snickered but didn't take his eyes off Baby Love. "He does look like Kendra."

"Right?" I nodded.

"But the vibe is all Tyrell," he added quietly.

It was the first time Leo had truly acknowledged Tyrell since this all began.

At the double funeral, he was solid as a rock—there for everyone, Tyrell's mom included. For me, he stood strong as I watched them lower Kendra's casket into the ground. Through all of it, I hadn't seen him shed a single tear.

The realization hit me like a ton of bricks. There was something in the way Leo looked at Baby Love—so lost in the moment, his focus unwavering—that broke my heart a little. My eyes stung with unshed tears.

"Are you good?" I asked softly.

Leo sniffled faintly, bobbing his head. "Yeah, I'm good."

I noticed around his eyes becoming red. Though my instinct was to ask more, I decided to leave it alone. When he was ready, he'd talk.

"Okay," I said, pointing toward the door with my thumb. "I'm gonna take that shower."

"Cool," he said, refocusing on Baby Love.

"You good with him? You got it?"

Leo glanced up at me and smiled. A genuine one. "I got it, Ivy League. Go 'head."

I rolled my eyes, which made him chuckle.

I looked down at Baby Love to see he'd already drifted off.

"I can put him in his crib—"

"He's good," Leo said, his eyes back on Baby Love. "Go on. Enjoy your shower."

* * *

2 weeks later…

I lay face down on my bed, one arm dangling off the edge of the mattress.

An itch on my back begged for attention, but I ignored it. Too tired to even scratch it.

Last night had been rough. Baby Love had been dealing with colic for the past week, and it only seemed to be getting worse.

The ringing of my phone on the nightstand interrupted my moment of stillness, and I groaned.

Lifting my head to see who was calling felt like too much effort.

The past few days had been grueling, but thankfully, I wasn't doing it alone. Leo had stepped up. After that night when I'd handed Baby Love to him in desperation for a shower, Leo had been more present than ever.

He'd grown more confident with holding Baby Love, no longer as nervous or unsure.

We were finally finding our rhythm when colic hit.

We'd discovered the issue during a late-night emergency call with Baby Love's doctor—a luxury made possible by the trust fund. Instead of taking him to a traditional office, we'd hired a doctor who made house calls. They assured us Baby Love was growing well and thriving.

But knowing didn't make those nights easier.

It was like clockwork. Midnight would strike, and Baby Love would cry. And cry. And cry. It didn't stop until dawn began breaking over the horizon.

Leo and I tag-teamed, rocking him for hours, taking turns dozing off and risking dropping him. Last night had been one of the hardest.

The phone stopped ringing, only to start again.

"What?" I groaned into my pillow. "Go away."

Finally having a chance to sleep, I didn't want to talk to anyone. Not even myself.

There was a concert scheduled for tonight. One I'd gone to every year for the past five years with Kendra, Tyrell, and Leo.

I hadn't even considered attending. I didn't have the energy to think about it, let alone make plans.

My phone started ringing for the third time.

At this point, I was too annoyed to ignore it. Begrudgingly, I lifted my head and reached for the phone. My arm felt like it weighed a hundred pounds.

Dragging my tired eyes to the screen, I saw a name that made me sit up straight in bed: *Mrs. Rachel Simmons.*

Kendra's mother.

"Mrs. Simmons, hello," I rasped into the phone, clearing my throat as I adjusted to a sitting position. "How are you?"

She chuckled softly on the other end of the line, pausing to catch her breath. "I feel like I should be asking *you* that."

I let out a weary laugh, dropping my head into my hands.

"How's it going over there?" she asked.

"Great," I lied. "We're all great."

"You don't sound it."

I inhaled deeply, closing my eyes tightly.

I had purposely avoided reaching out to the Simmons. They were still grieving the loss of their daughter, and the last thing I wanted was to burden them with our struggles. Leo and I were grieving, too, but it wasn't the same. This was something we had to figure out ourselves.

"I'm just a little tired," I admitted. "We had a very fun night last night. And yes, I am being sarcastic."

Mrs. Simmons burst into laughter, and despite my exhaustion, I found myself chuckling along.

"Lawd, it's been a long while, but I remember those nights very well," she said warmly. "What is it? Y'all sleep training? Is he teething? Got gas?"

"Colic," I said with a nod, even though she couldn't see me. "That godforsaken colic."

She giggled knowingly.

I frowned as I rubbed my aching eyes. "I don't understand how he can cry for so long without running out of breath."

"*Mmm-hmm*," she murmured, the understanding clear in her tone.

"He's been colicky for a whole week now. Always at night, for three straight hours," I explained. "Then he falls asleep for maybe fifteen minutes before he's up again. He finally went down an hour ago."

"Well, why didn't you call us?"

Her question made me pause. My gaze wandered across my room, landing on my high-tech workstation. The multiple screens sat untouched, reminders of the professional life I'd barely had time to consider since Baby Love entered my world.

"Myself, Walt, and Tyrell's mom all told you that if you ever needed anything, you could call us," she said gently.

"I know," I admitted quietly. "It's just... you're still grieving. And while Leo and I are, too, it's not the same as what you and Tyrell's mom are going through. If the hardest thing for us right now is dealing with a lack of sleep, we can handle it."

"But you don't *have* to, Ivy," she said firmly. "We were prepared to help Kendra and Tyrell the moment they told us they were having a baby, and we want to be that help for you and Leo. You don't have to do this alone."

Her words hit me square in the chest.

"The baby needs you two at your best," she continued. "And if you need a break to rest, tell us. We're here for you. The saying 'it takes a village' is more than just a saying. If you're depleted, let us help."

I exhaled a shaky breath, her reassurances sinking in.

"Would you like us to take the baby today?"

My head shot up at her offer. "Would you?"

She laughed softly.

"I mean..." I cleared my throat, pressing a hand to my chest to steady myself. "It's so last minute, Mrs. Simmons. I couldn't ask y'all to—"

"We'd love to," she said, her voice kind. "We'd absolutely love an opportunity to spend time with..." She paused, then asked, "What's his name?"

I bit the inside of my cheek, cringing. "We haven't chosen a name yet."

"Oh."

"It's just..." I started, feeling the weight of my hesitation. "Kendra wanted it to be a surprise. She never told us or you guys what name she was considering, and I don't want to pick just anything."

"It's okay," Mrs. Simmons said quickly. "You're doing great. You *two* are doing great."

"We've been calling him Baby Love," I said, a small smile tugging at my lips. "You know, Baby, and Kendra and Tyrell's last name."

She chuckled. "That's clever. A good placeholder until you decide."

I nodded to myself.

"Look," she continued, "Walt and I can be on the road in half an hour and at your place in about an hour. We can pick up... Baby Love, is it?"

I smiled. "Yup. Baby Love."

She giggled again. "We'll take him for the weekend and bring him back Monday. Does that work?"

"Like a dream," I admitted, my voice breathless with relief.

"Wonderful," she said warmly. "We'll start getting ready now."

"Thank you so much, Mrs. Simmons. I'll have everything ready when you get here. Is there anything specific I should pack in his bag?"

"Nothing at all. Whatever he needs, we'll take care of it."

I felt a rush of gratitude wash over me as I pictured uninterrupted sleep for the first time in weeks.

"We'll see you soon," she said before hanging up.

Springing to my feet, I headed straight for Leo's room.

I knocked lightly at first, then a little harder when I got no response.

"Go away, Ivy," Leo mumbled, his voice muffled.

Ignoring him, I opened the door to find him lying face down in his pillow, his long limbs hanging off the edge of his bed.

"Ivy, please get out—"

"Mrs. Simmons just called," I interrupted. "She and Mr. Simmons are coming to pick up Baby Love for the weekend."

Leo's head shot up so fast, I thought it might fly off.

"They'll be here in half an hour," I said, grinning. "All we have to do is get Baby Love ready—"

"Say less," Leo said, jumping out of bed.

"Wait," I said, stopping him mid-stride. "Shouldn't we decide what to pack?"

"What?" Leo threw his hands up dramatically and spun to face me. "No. Pack *everything*. Throw it all in the bag." He held his thumb and index finger close together, his expression exaggerated. "I'm *this* close to throwing Baby Love in the car before they even park."

"Leo!"

He raised his hands in mock surrender. "Look, I love the kid, but I'm tired. So…" He tilted his head toward the nursery. "Let's get him ready, ship him out for the weekend, and then I'm crashing. Straight to sleep."

I laughed as I followed him back to Baby Love's nursery, his long strides easily outpacing mine. "Same."

* * *

"You ready?" Leo called from my bedroom door.

I stood in front of my full-length mirror, sliding the final earring into place.

"Yeah," I replied, brushing a hand over my high bun to ensure it was smooth. "Just need a few more minutes."

"Aight," Leo said, lingering in the doorway. "The car will be here in fifteen."

With Baby Love safely with Kendra's parents and a glorious seven hours of uninterrupted sleep behind me, I was ready for a much-needed night out.

The *Back in the Day Bash* was a tradition. Every year when the 90s R&B concert rolled through Manhattan, Kendra, Tyrell, Leo, and I made a night of it. We shared a love for 90s music that bonded us, and this was the event we never missed.

Tonight was different. It was my first concert without Kendra and Tyrell.

Satisfied with my look, I nodded, pleased I kept it simple. A cropped leather jacket over a knotted graphic tee featuring Aaliyah's face, black leggings, and knee-high boots. This was my usual concert attire, a nod to my love for 90s R&B and to Kendra, who always said I could never go wrong with that outfit because I resembled the singer which always made me blush.

Leo reappeared in the doorway, his voice interrupting my thoughts. "Our driver's five minutes away. You ready?"

He looked effortlessly cool in a brown suede shearling bomber jacket over a plain black tee, paired with black jeans and black-and-white Nike Air Jordans. His closet was practically a shrine to Jordans—he owned every pair imaginable.

"Yes, I'm ready," I said, grabbing my crossbody bag.

"You look nice," he said, his gaze lingering a little longer than usual.

I frowned playfully. "I wear the same thing every year. *You* used to call it my 'concert uniform.' Remember? You tease me about it every year relentlessly."

He shrugged. "It looks good on you this year."

I stared at him for a moment, noting the smirk tugging at his lips before he turned and headed downstairs.

"Weirdo," I said, trying to hide the blush creeping into my cheeks.

I couldn't explain it, but things felt different with Leo lately.

* * *

On the drive to the venue, we checked in with Kendra's parents to make sure Baby Love was doing well. True to his routine, he had fallen asleep right on time. I just hoped the Simmons could handle his colic when it inevitably hit in a few hours.

"Earth to Ivy," Leo's voice cut through my thoughts.

I turned to find him staring at me, an amused expression on his face.

"Where the hell did you go?" he asked with a laugh.

I chuckled, shaking my head. "I was just thinking about the baby."

His brows furrowed slightly.

"His colic," I clarified. "And whether the Simmons will—"

"They've got it," Leo interrupted with a snicker. "They have way more experience with babies than we do."

"I know, but they're older, and—"

"They've got it," he repeated, cutting me off again. Then, grinning mischievously, he reached over and took my head in his hands, giving it a playful shake. "Clear that head of yours. Empty it just this once."

I shoved him away, emphasizing it with a glare, which only made him laugh harder.

"Tonight is about fun," he said, his tone lighter as he settled back into his seat. "Reconnecting to baby-less Leo and Ivy. Let's enjoy it. Let's get it!"

The streets of Manhattan buzzed with energy as our driver pulled up near the venue's private entrance. The vibrant lights of midtown seemed to reflect the excitement building inside me.

Perks of being friends with an NBA player meant we bypassed the lines and went straight to the standing area by the stage. It was prime real estate for the concert, and as soon as I stepped into the arena, the familiar thrill of the *Back in the Day Bash* washed over me.

The DJ was spinning 90s classics while the crowd eagerly awaited the acts. I could feel the pulse of anticipation in the air, but something was missing.

Kendra.

Her absence was glaring, and for a moment, the joy of the evening dimmed.

"Here," Leo said, pulling me out of my thoughts.

He handed me a clear plastic cup filled with a bright orange-yellow drink, ice cubes floating on top.

"What is it?" I shouted over the music.

He leaned close, his breath warm against my ear. "Tequila sunrise."

I couldn't help but grin. "Why would you give me tequila when you know tequila and I don't mix?"

"Because," Leo said, raising his voice to be heard over the music, "you need to loosen up tonight. Get your mind right." He brought the tequila sunrise closer to me with a knowing smirk. "Take it, toss it back, and let's get live, Ivy League."

I clicked my tongue, unable to stop the smile forming on my lips.

As much as I hated that nickname when he first started teasing me with it, hearing it now softened my mood.

It didn't take long for the combination of one tequila sunrise and two shots of tequila to melt away my reservations. Sad thoughts floated to the back of my mind, replaced by a warm buzz and a surge of uninhibited energy.

The arena pulsed with the bass of 90s R&B, and I let the music take over, swinging my hips and losing myself in the moment.

For the first time in what felt like forever, I was truly having fun again.

Leo and I danced like we had at every concert we attended over the years. When Kendra and Tyrell were with us, they'd always pair off. On nights like those, Leo was my default dance partner whenever I wasn't dancing with a stranger. And he was good—great, even. For someone who towered over me, his rhythm was impressive, and he could always keep up with the beat.

Everything was perfect—until it wasn't.

As the intermission began, the DJ spun Groove Theory's "Tell Me," and it hit me like a freight train.

The song was *ours*, Kendra's and mine. We'd sing it together, off-key but full of joy, every time it played. It was a staple of this concert, a moment we always shared. Hearing it now brought those memories rushing back, too powerful to resist.

I closed my eyes, swaying to the beat as tears welled up behind my lids. I mouthed the lyrics, hating the ache in my chest but cherishing the bittersweet memories they brought.

I felt arms wrap around me from behind, the familiar scent of Leo's cologne reaching me before he spoke.

"Don't start crying on me now," he whispered in my ear, pulling me closer.

I let my weight fall into him, turning to bury my face in his chest. His black tee soaked up my tears, likely smudging my makeup, but I didn't care.

The music thundered around us, drowning out the sound of my quiet sobs as Leo held me steady through the song.

When it ended, I pulled away, wiping at my damp cheeks and trying to collect myself.

"You good now?" Leo asked, crouching slightly so we were eye level.

I nodded and managed a small, "Yeah."

He studied me for a moment before pointing toward the bar reserved for premium standing area ticket holders. "I'm gonna get you another drink."

I waved my hand, shaking my head. "I think I've had enough."

A smirk tugged at his lips. "No such thing."

I laughed despite myself.

The rest of the concert went smoothly—no more tears, just good vibes and even better music. By the end, I felt like a different person, lighter, freer.

When Leo suggested we hit up an after-party at a club, I surprised myself by agreeing.

The event was held at *Club Déjà Vu.*

Clubs weren't usually my scene. They were too loud, too crowded, too much. But VIP was a different story.

Up in the private section, the music felt less overwhelming, and the energy was more intimate. With drinks flowing and good music keeping the night alive, I let go even further.

"See? Look at you," Leo said, his smile wide and his eyes glossy from the liquor. "Already looking better."

I giggled, shaking my head. "Leo, I'm so drunk right now, I don't know my up from my down."

"Perfect," he replied, grabbing another shot from the table. "And when we're done here, you get to go home and sleep to your heart's content. It's a good night."

I leaned back in my seat, laughing softly.

"Leo Vanguard," a voice interrupted.

We turned to see a sharply dressed man approaching our table.

His tailored suit screamed money, and his cologne preceded him by a mile.

"I'm Vincenzo Rinaldi, owner of Club Déjà Vu," the man said, extending a hand to Leo. "Pleasure to finally meet you."

"Same here," Leo said, shaking his hand firmly.

"I spotted you as soon as you walked into the club from my office. Couldn't miss you," Vincenzo said, gesturing toward the club's main stage. "Would it be too much to ask for you to say a few words on the mic?"

Leo shook his head, pointing to the drinks on the table. "I don't think I'm in any state to say anything into a mic right now."

"How about at a price?" Vincenzo countered, flashing a perfect smile. "Five grand. Five words, six max."

I choked.

Five thousand dollars? U.S. dollars?

"Six grand, six words," Leo countered, "and I'll shake your hand."

"Fifty-five hundred," Vincenzo said next, "a handshake and your next drinks on me."

Leo grinned. "Six grand, I'll shake your hand, I'll continue to pay for my own drinks, and I'll even take a photo with you. Final offer."

"Deal," Vincenzo said, shaking Leo's hand again.

Before I knew it, we were whisked off to a private office at the back of the club. Drinks were poured, papers were signed, and a thick envelope exchanged hands.

Minutes later, Leo was on stage, riling up the crowd with a few words that had them roaring with excitement. A photo op with Vincenzo followed before we were back in VIP, laughing about the surreal turn of events.

The liquor in my system had gone from energizing to sedating, and my feet ached from dancing all night in heels. I was ready to call it a night.

Leo called for our car, and within minutes, we were on our way home, the city lights fading behind us.

In the back seat, we were on our way back home to Greene

Gardens when I said, "You just went to a club for an after-party but got paid six thousand dollars just to say less than two sentences on a microphone," I said to Leo in the car. "What the hell?"

He grinned beside me, his dimple making a rare appearance. "What the heaven, actually."

I laughed, and he joined in, his chuckle low and rich, vibrating in the quiet of the car.

"Does that happen often?" I asked, my curiosity piqued.

He nodded, slinging his head back against the headrest. "All the time. That's why I love the club."

I turned to study him for a moment. His Adam's apple bobbed every time he swallowed, and the motion kept me mesmerized.

"That NBA check can go but so far," he added, his eyes still closed, his voice lazy with weariness and tequila. "So I gotta... what they say? Supplement the income? My name is hot right now and it's not gonna be hot forever. So every chance I get, I'm cashing in."

I don't know if it was the liquor or life lately, but Leo was looking different to me these days. He was always handsome—that much was a given. But I guess I'd never seen him outside of his unserious nature. Always behaving like life was a game. Tonight, though, at the club, the way he negotiated at the drop of a hat with such ease and confidence... it was magnetic. Attractive.

He turned his head, still resting back, to look at me. "What's up?"

"Huh?" I stammered, caught off guard.

A small smile tugged at his lips before he licked them, his tongue gliding slowly over his lower lip. "You're staring."

"Oh." I blinked, dragging my eyes away immediately. "Was I?"

"*Mm-hmm,*" he murmured.

"Sorry."

"No need to apologize... Ivy League." His tone was soft, teasing, but laced with something heavier, deeper, that I couldn't quite name.

I turned my head slowly to look at him again, only to find him wearing a smile unlike any he'd given me before. It wasn't mischievous or mocking—it was... intimate. Like he saw right through me and could read my thoughts.

Leo was always poking fun at me, centering on how uptight I was—a fact he didn't know was one of my deepest insecurities. What I wouldn't give to be able to let loose all the time, to embrace the kind of freedom he lived with daily.

But his smile tonight? It didn't poke or prod. It didn't belittle or tease. It felt like it was just for me. Warm. Knowing. And his eyes—they held something I hadn't seen before.

His gaze fell to my lips, and I instinctively licked them, a nervous habit I couldn't stop even if I tried.

The sound that escaped him was low, guttural—barely audible—but it shot through me like lightning. A zing sparked between my thighs, and I shifted in my seat to soothe the sensation. His eyes followed the movement, trailing from my lips to my neck, down to my chest, where they lingered on the rise and fall of my breasts. The weight of his gaze was like a touch, hot and possessive.

When his eyes finally lifted to mine again, they smoldered, even in the dim light of the backseat. My breathing hitched, coming faster and heavier, and I couldn't tear my gaze from his.

What the fuck was happening? Was it the liquor? It had to be the liquor.

Because why else would his attention on me have such a powerful effect?

I shut my eyes and cleared my throat, then turned to face forward, pulling my focus away from him as though it might shield me from the fire he'd ignited.

"Whoa," I whispered to myself, exhaling all the air in my lungs in one shaky breath.

"Fuck," Leo muttered beside me, his voice thick, before releasing a deep breath of his own. "We definitely drank way too damn much tonight."

"Yup," I replied, my eyes fixed on the driver's headrest, refusing to look at him again.

The rest of the ride home passed in tense silence. The kind of silence that could shatter with a single wrong word or look.

What the hell was happening? My life felt like it was in free fall. My best friend was gone, I was responsible for her baby, and now Leo had me shifting in my seat to calm the thumping ache he'd caused behind the seat of my panties with nothing more than a look.

When our driver pulled up to the curb in front of the house, I let out a sigh of relief, pushed open my back door and got out of the car desperate for the safety of distance.

Once inside, I wasted no time. I bolted for the stairs before Leo could even close the door.

"I'll see you in the morning," I called over my shoulder when I was halfway up.

"Aight," he said, his voice trailing behind me. "Good night."

The moment my bedroom door clicked shut, I began peeling off my clothes as I moved toward my bathroom. My skin felt too hot, my pulse too erratic, my thoughts racing too fast.

Sex hadn't crossed my mind in years. My career had been my sole focus. That anchor seat at *Free-Throw Nation* was all I'd cared about. But now? Now, after that ride home, I was under the cold spray of my shower, gritting my teeth as the frigid water bit into my skin. Anything to cool the fire raging within me.

Unfortunately, the cold did little to help.

Later, lying naked in my bed, my face buried in my pillow, I gave in. My fingers found my pleasure point between lower lips, and I rubbed myself to the memory of Leo's smoldering gaze, the sound of his moan, and the way his attention set my body aflame.

When the release finally came, it was shattering, leaving me trembling and breathless. But even as I drifted into sleep, his face stayed with me, haunting my dreams.

"OH MY GOD," I heard shouted as I ducked my head into the waiting black car. "It's Leo Vanguard!"

The screams followed immediately. Through the closed door, the sound was muffled but still distinct—a mix of excitement and adoration from the fans gathered near the Bronx Metro Arena barricade. I raised a hand to wave at the group through the tinted, lowered window, acknowledging their presence before my driver raised the window.

Even though the Bronx Ballers' player entrance was separate from the main one, die-hard fans always seemed to figure out where to wait for glimpses of their favorite players.

The driver pulled off a moment later, and as we merged onto the street, my phone began to chime. I glanced down at the screen, and a smile tugged at my lips when I saw who was calling.

"Simeon," I greeted as I answered. "What's up, man?"

"Everything as always, LV," he replied, his voice upbeat. "How about you? How are you?"

"As good as I'm gonna be, I guess."

"Aw, not the response I'd want to hear from a winner."

I chuckled, the sound easing some of the tension from my shoulders.

Simeon King was my agent and had been since 2023. He was sharp and no-nonsense, with a knack for making even the most daunting situations feel manageable.

"I caught your game against the Pistons," he continued. "Good game. I see those extra morning hours in the gym have you stalking that court like a beast."

I chuckled.

"No balls from the other team are getting past you, LV," he added, chuckling. "I like it."

"Well, I love it," I replied, leaning back against the seat as the streets of New York blurred past the window.

I was missing the city already. Ivy and I had been living in Greene Gardens for almost two months now, and the place still didn't feel like home. Every chance I got to come back to NYC, any borough—even for just a game—I took it.

I wasn't like Ivy. It was hard for me to spend all my days and nights in that village.

The thought of Ivy brought my mind back to that morning after the concert.

"Good morning," I greeted as Ivy stepped into the kitchen.

Her steps faltered for a split second when she saw me sitting at the table. I wasn't sure if she was surprised I was up so early or if she was thinking about what had happened—or almost happened—the night before.

"Hey," she said, her voice forced. "Good morning."

She moved toward the cabinet, pulling down a mug to make her coffee. Her shoulders were tense, her movements stiff—classic Ivy when something was on her mind.

"How'd you sleep?" I asked, breaking the silence.

"Good," she replied quickly, her eyes carefully avoiding mine. "You?"

"Great," I said with a smirk.

I knew she had to have slept well because I'd heard her moaning in her room shortly after we'd said good night.

The night of the concert had been... different. Ivy and I had gone to the same event every year with Kendra and Tyrell, but this time, something had shifted. And it wasn't just because Kendra and Tyrell weren't there. It was the way Ivy and I had interacted—the tension between us that felt new and uncharted.

For years, Ivy and I had known we weren't each other's type. She was meticulous, uptight, and far too serious for my free-spirited, live-in-the-moment personality. We'd agreed early on that whatever our friends had in mind for us just wasn't going to work.

But last night changed something.

When she raced upstairs after we got home, I decided to give her some space. But when I stood outside her door, prepared to knock, I heard her moaning on the other side. And instead of walking away like I should have, I stood there, frozen, listening until the sound stopped.

When I returned to my room, I was wound tighter than a spring, my dick hard, body tense with something I couldn't shake.

"We should talk about last night," I said now, breaking the silence in the kitchen.

Ivy froze mid-pour, then slowly set the coffee pot down before turning to face me.

"What about last night?" she asked cautiously.

"The ride home."

Her gaze flicked over me briefly before she looked away again. "We had a lot to drink," she said, raising a hand to cut me off. "And we've been through a lot. Sometimes that makes people act... differently."

"Ivy—"

"Let's not let what happened—or didn't happen—change our rela-tionship," she interjected, her tone firm. "Okay?"

I leaned back in my chair, studying her. She was trying so hard to put this wall back up between us, but I knew the truth. Whatever she wanted to pretend hadn't happened last night—it was already too late to undo.

"Aight," I said finally, forcing a casual nod.

"Okay," she said, turning back to the coffeemaker. "Because we need to stay focused on Baby Love and all of our responsibilities."

I tried to listen, but my eyes had other plans, trailing down her frame. Her legs, her hips... everything about her was distracting in a way it never had been before.

Whatever Ivy thought about keeping things the same between us, I knew one thing for sure: there was no going back.

"How are things at home?" Simeon asked, pulling me back to the present. "How's life in Greene Gardens?"

"Still adjusting, man," I admitted with a shake of my head. "Still adjusting."

"You know my parents supply the market out there with produce."

My brows shot up. "Oh, word?"

"Yeah." He chuckled. "I brokered the deal for them."

"Why does that not surprise me?" I said with a grin.

We laughed together, the sound easing some of the weight on my chest.

"And Ivy?" Simeon asked next. "How has living with her and raising...*umm...hmm*. I'm sorry, I don't believe I know the baby's name."

I chuckled. "We don't either, man."

There was silence on the line, which made me laugh a little harder.

"Simeon, it's a long story," I told him. "Just know we're trying to figure that out along with other things, too."

He snickered. "Oh, I can imagine."

"Ivy has adjusted more than me, though," I added. "She just... gets it. She's a fast learner. You would think she's been training to take care of a baby at the last minute all her life. She's amazing, Simeon."

"Hmph."

"I don't know where I'd be without her," I admitted, a smile tugging at my lips. "She's a good partner. A great one."

"If I didn't know any better, I'd think you were talking like a man in love, LV," Simeon teased with a chuckle.

I scoffed and laughed. "Man, what?"

"I don't know," he said. "I just sense something in your voice. You sound different talking about her today."

I shook my head. "Nah." I laughed again, brushing it off. "If you only knew how opposite Ivy and I are, you'd never say that. We could never happen."

"Well," Simeon started, "never say never. Being opposites isn't a dealbreaker in a lot of cases. It can be the greatest attraction. Me and Eryn are a testament to that. She and I are very, very different, but I married her, and she's carrying my baby, and I'm the happiest man on this planet."

I rubbed my lips together, his words making me pause.

"Don't sleep on the idea that being opposites could work," Simeon added. "In the grand scheme of things, it might mean very little, you know?"

"Yeah," I replied, though the thought lingered.

But how true was that for Ivy and me?

"Anyway," Simeon said, his tone shifting. "We're getting a little off track from the reason for my call."

I blinked, refocusing. "Go ahead."

"I've got that extra stream of income you've been looking for," he revealed. "And it's something you already told me you love doing."

My brows shot up. "Word?"

I've been pushing Simeon to help me figure out how to grow that sign-on bonus from the Ballers. I ain't about wasting money on nonsense. I want to make sure I've got something solid lined up for when I retire.

One of Simeon's first clients, Dallas Roque, who played for the Oakland Flames, had exactly that—a sports nutrition brand growing exponentially. I wanted something similar. Anything, really.

One of my reasons for signing with Simeon was so he could help me secure a business deal or start something of my own that wouldn't leave me relying solely on balling for income. He promised he had me and told me all I needed was an idea—he'd handle the rest. The problem was, I didn't have solid ideas. Just random suggestions. But he stayed patient.

Over the summer, I'd mentioned my love of LEGO, and he assured me he'd figure something out. Was this it?

"Word," Simeon said with a chuckle. "And this potential extra stream is a good one, LV. A great one."

* * *

Ivy lifted her glass across from me, wearing a big smile.

I snickered, reaching for mine and lifting it too.

We were at dinner in Manhattan at the late hour of 9 p.m.

The Simmons had been kind enough to ask if they could spend another weekend with Baby Love, and Ivy and I couldn't get him packed up fast enough. With free time and a craving for something other than takeout, we drove to the city to celebrate my good news with a proper meal.

"To you and your new deal," Ivy toasted, her voice warm and proud. "I am so happy and proud of you."

I clinked my glass with hers, my smile almost hurting my cheeks. "Thank you, thank you. And cheers to you."

She laughed.

"For racking up over 10,000 subscribers because you were talking your shit."

She giggled, shaking her head. "Please. I really think they subscribed because I was holding Baby Love."

I pushed my glass closer to hers. "Ivy, you better take this clink, woman."

That made her laugh even harder.

This week had felt lighter. two months into guardianship, we were finally finding our rhythm. Baby Love was sleeping better, the colic had passed, and while Ivy hadn't returned to on-court press, she'd found her groove at home.

She finally obliged, clinking her glass with mine before bringing her champagne to her lips.

We were at Verde Vista, an upscale eatery in Manhattan's historic district. Greene Gardens didn't have any restaurants yet, thank God. Although our living situation was starting to feel normal, Greene Gardens didn't feel like home. It simply wasn't Manhattan. Not even close.

"I got another thousand subscribers earlier today," she said, unable to hide her pride. "But I don't know if they tuned in for me or the cute baby I had to hold while recording."

I chuckled.

A week ago, after a game against the Pistons, Ivy had been so pissed at the refs that she fired up her phone and recorded a video ranting about the bad calls. Most of her frustration centered on the unfair treatment I'd been getting. It went viral, and she gained thousands of subscribers overnight. It even caught the attention of her network. There were talks of giving her a sports commentary web series.

"I just hope they don't expect me to always be holding a baby," she added, setting her glass down. "Because that was totally not the plan."

"Sometimes the best things aren't planned," I said with a grin. "Spontaneity is the spice of life."

"Yeah, yeah." She waved me off. "Enough about that. Tell me more about this very lucrative deal, sir."

I smiled, biting my bottom lip.

She and I had already ordered our food, but it hadn't arrived yet. That was fine. Between training and traveling, we hadn't had time to catch up.

"It's called Leo Vanguard's Championship Court," I began, sitting up straighter. "It's a signature basketball court set I'll help develop. Complete with figures that look like me and my teammates, LEGO spectators, scoreboards, and court markings. It's mad detailed." I shook my head, smiling wider. "They showed me a replica model that almost had me forgetting who the fuck I was in their office, Ivy."

She hollered a laugh.

"The model had this section of stands that was dedicated to my fans. The LEGO figures had on basketball jerseys with my name and number on the back. It was crazy."

"Wow," she whispered, her eyes wide with genuine amazement. "That is so dope. I might even consider playing with them Legos like you do."

My smile dropped as I pointed at her. "See, I done already told you I don't play with Legos. I build them."

She smirked. "*Mm-hmm.*"

The restaurant had an intimate, garden-like atmosphere, with lush plants and tropical flowers decorating the space. The soft lighting and gentle music in the background created a serene vibe that kept Ivy and me speaking in soft tones.

"So, like," she said, leaning in with an eager expression, "what's the actual deal? Is it just the set?"

"Nah," I replied. "And that's what makes this shit even better. The deal includes an upfront endorsement fee, royalties from the sales of the basketball sets and mini figures, appearances at events, and possibly a percentage of revenues from related digital content."

"Oh my God, Leo!" she exclaimed, her excitement contagious.

"Simeon did his big one for me on this shit, for real." I beamed. "The contract specified commitments like social media promotion, participation in video and photo shoots for commercials or what-ever, and appearances at LEGO stores or trade shows. But I'm already at those places anyway."

"'Cause you genuinely love playing with Legos," she teased, her tone playful.

I gave her a hard blank stare.

She tossed her head back in laughter, which made me kiss my teeth.

"Seriously though," she said, holding up a hand as her laughter faded into a grin. "This is so damn dope and inspiring. You got a deal working with a brand you actually love and getting a product made in your likeness that you already have experience using. That is so ideal and perfect. I hope you know that."

"Oh, I know it." I nodded. "It feels good."

"It should."

"I'm just happy Simeon talked me out of getting into the business of making umbrellas because what the fuck was I thinking?" I shook my head.

Ivy snickered, holding a smile on her lips as her eyes locked onto mine.

I stared at her for a moment, genuinely happy to be celebrating this milestone with her and grateful for this time together.

Her smile was still in place as she squinted her eyes at me. "What?"

I wasn't sure what was happening, but being around Ivy was different these days. So very different.

Since that night of the concert—and hearing her in her room, moaning like crazy after whatever moment we had in the car ride home—she hasn't looked the same to me.

Weeks before that, I started noticing things I'd somehow missed before. Her legs, long and toned, and the way her curves filled out a simple tee and shorts. Ivy was always meticulous about her appearance. Everything had to be just right. But lately, she seemed freer, more natural.

Even tonight. Because our decision to come to the city was so last-minute, she didn't have time to get fully dolled up. She wore a casual sweater, jeans, and a messy bun at the top of her head, her lips slick with nothing but gloss. And yet, she looked absolutely stunning.

"Nothing," I answered, forcing my eyes off her. "Just thinking."

"About?"

I would never say anything close to the truth. She already made it clear the night of the concert—and again the morning after—that we should keep things the way they were for Baby Love's sake. And I agreed.

I didn't have the best track record with relationships. Most women I dealt with knew the deal—fun with no strings. Vanessa, a lady friend I hadn't spoken to in weeks, had been blowing up my phone complaining about how unavailable I'd become. Between my career, Baby Love, and everything else, I didn't have the energy to entertain anything more.

"About how Kendra and Tyrell would love this right now," I said instead.

It wasn't what I wanted to say, but it was still the truth.

Ivy snorted a laugh. "Oh, they would have been beside themselves. You and I going out to dinner together? Just us two, and on purpose?"

I hollered a laugh. "And not just having dinner because they ditched us to go hook up in the car."

"A car we all took to get to where they said we should all hang out, only to leave us alone," Ivy added, shaking her head.

"Yo!" I laughed, bringing my fist to my lips. "I used to *hate* when they did that shit. Fuck in the car we had to ride back to campus in."

"And *never* air that bitch out before we got in it. *Ugh!*" Ivy gritted her teeth, then busted out laughing. "I wanted to hurt them every time."

"They loved them some cars, man."

"Yeah," Ivy whispered, her smile fading into a frown, her chin trembling as tears welled in her eyes.

The sight hit me hard, a pang tightening my chest.

I sighed and reached across the table to take her hand. She started patting her eyes dry with the other, and when our gazes met, a smile broke through the sadness on her lips.

At that moment, our server arrived with our food. Ivy composed herself quickly, and once I was sure she was okay, I leaned back in my seat.

"Sometimes," she said, picking up her fork from the cup of hot water with lemon she had asked for upon arrival, "the only comfort I find in all this is knowing they died together. Because I just know..."

"Neither of them would've been able to live without the other," I finished, nodding in agreement.

"Yup." Ivy inhaled deeply, letting the breath out slowly. "I just wonder when I'm going to stop damn near breaking down every time I think about them. Every time I think about *her*."

After eating, sharing a little more conversation, and settling the bill, Ivy and I made our way out to the waiting car.

The drive back to Greene Gardens was quiet, a few comments exchanged about how Manhattan felt different to Ivy after being away for sometime.

It was bittersweet, more bitter than sweet, leaving the city. It felt like leaving home for somewhere that didn't quite feel like home yet.

When we finally stepped inside the house, Ivy flicked on the table light by the front door and began slipping off her heels and peeling off her jacket.

"That was fun," she said to me, hooking her coat on the coat rack. "Thanks for insisting we eat out and not just drive to the nearest town for takeout."

"They really should get to opening some restaurants around here, though, damn," I said, peeling off my jacket and placing it on the coat rack beside Ivy's. "They got the space."

"They're working on it," Ivy said. "They have a community board they've put together. Brand new. I'm thinking about joining it."

"Hmph."

"Anyway." She smiled, walking up to me and wrapping her arms around my waist. "Thank you, LV."

Ivy was much shorter than me at her five-foot-four height, so her hugs were always from my lower half.

I leaned forward to wrap my arms around her too.

The embrace, as always, started as a friendly gesture, but after a few seconds, it didn't feel that way.

Neither one of us let go after a few seconds, choosing to just stand there.

And it felt right. Feeling her body against mine, the gentle thump of her heartbeat too.

It was comforting. Something I didn't realize I needed in that moment—or that I even wanted more of.

I flattened my hand against her back and heard a soft moan escape through her lips.

The moan reminded me of the sounds she was making in her room the night of the concert. How much I wanted to be one with that door so I could hear her clearer because the little that I could hear sounded so damn good.

Without a second thought, I tightened my arms around her back, and she simply melted against me.

For sure, this hug was unlike any other quick embrace Ivy and I had ever done. Because having her close and for the amount of time she was close to me, it started to have an effect on my body. Inside and out.

The moment I felt myself hardening in my jeans, Ivy noticed it too. Because Ivy pulled away slightly, which made me pull away too. And the second we created enough space between us and looked at each other, I noticed the look in her eyes... was different.

Though we were no longer hugging per se, she was still in my arms, in my space, and me in hers. Our chests were starting to show how heavy we were breathing. Ivy darted her eyes along mine as she inhaled a trembling breath through her lips.

What the hell was going on? Why did I not want to create even more space between us? Why did I want to eliminate the space that was there?

I lowered my attention to her lips, wanting to know what they felt like. Curious if they felt as good as they looked in that instance.

And just like that, Ivy shut her eyes, holding them closed tightly, then dropped her forehead against my ribs. "Oh, my God," she whispered.

"Ivy—"

"*Shh*," she shushed. "Please don't say anything right now."

She stepped back next, creating space between us until there was enough space between us to help me think straight again.

"*Umm*," she whispered to herself. "Shit."

I couldn't say anything. Didn't want to. Too confused and sure at the same time. Confused at the fact that I wanted to kiss my friend and still wanted to kiss her. Sure that I was officially not seeing my friend as just a friend but as something else.

She pointed up the stairs. "I'm... going to take advantage of being childfree tonight and get some sleep."

All I could do was nod.

And in my silence, she shut her eyes and turned to walk away, stopping just before turning to face me again, then turning to face the stairs once more.

As if she were having a dispute in her head, contemplating if she should go or stay, as I stood there, genuinely stunned.

"Shit, Leo," she expressed, dropping her arms at her side. "What the hell is happening right now between us? Like... what?"

I parted my lips to say something. "I... I..."

I simply couldn't think of anything to say in that moment.

"Fuck," she whispered, then grunted, pressing her hands to her face as she turned to climb the stairs. "Good night."

"Good night," I whispered to myself.

Shit.

So much for focusing on our responsibilities and not allowing our relationship to change... because what the hell was even that?

ivy

I SIGHED as my eyes peeled open and were met with darkness. I took a deep breath a second later, my eyes moving around my room in search of something familiar.

Two months in, and I still woke up in my bed wondering where the hell I was.

I sat up slowly, twisting my head to my right. Reaching for my phone a breath later, I pressed the device's side button to light up the screen to check the time. It was 3:03 in the morning. I had been getting up at the same time since moving out to Greene Gardens.

I pinched the inner corners of my eyes and kicked off the bedding covering me.

Like most nights, when I'd awaken in the middle of the night, I decided to take a trip to the kitchen to grab a drink of water and check on Baby Love before returning to my room to force myself to go back to sleep.

Baby Love had been sleeping really well. Truthfully, I was too before moving out here and having to take care of him. His waking in the middle of the night his first month in the house was handled by the baby nurse we hired. But when her time was up, and it was up to

Leo and me... mostly me, getting up in the middle of the night seemed to throw off my circadian rhythm. Because now, without even trying, and long after Baby Love was sleep-trained to perfection, sleeping practically through the night, I was still getting up at 3 a.m.

I took quiet steps down to the kitchen to grab a bottle of water, spotting Leo's sneakers neatly set to the side by the shoe rack.

He had gotten better at cleaning up after himself and keeping things in order around the house, when he was home.

Though he had gotten better with chipping in with his time and energy to raise the baby, he still had his obligations, especially now that he signed on to the LEGO brand and agreed to partner with them to develop his limited edition set.

I was happy for him, even when my career was looking like a dream deferred these days. The YouTube channel I'd treated like a side hustle for the longest was thriving, all because of that one video of me going in on a referee while rocking an infant to sleep.

After grabbing that drink of water, I headed upstairs with plans to stop at Baby Love's room, then retire in mine.

Baby Love. We still hadn't decided what his name would be. It was almost embarrassing at this point. We could have chosen any damn name, but shit, I just didn't want to.

I really wish Kendra told me what names she and Tyrell were considering. If I had a guiding post, I would feel more comfortable naming this child.

Baby Love's nursery was between my room and Leo's room. I stopped at the baby's door and pushed it open as quietly as I could. I spotted him lying on his back with his tiny fists up, framing his little face that was turned to his right.

Couldn't help my heart from melting at the sight of him in rest. It's crazy. When my colleagues at *Free-Throw Nation* who were also parents, discussed their children or insisted on showing me a random photo of their daughters or sons, I couldn't understand the fascination and how it was so immense they felt the need to share. I had never been around children before Baby Love. Before Kendra, no one I knew was having babies or even thinking about having them. We were all looking to grow in our careers. As I stared at Baby Love sound asleep in the crib we transitioned him into before he could outgrow his baby bassinet, I totally understood the craze for babies.

I smiled as I closed the door gently, positioning my feet to return to my bedroom.

But then I heard something. Couldn't be too sure at first if it was what I thought it was.

There was sniffing, then sobbing. Soft sobbing that sounded muffled and muted a little behind a closed door.

I turned in the direction of it, my eyes scanning the short hall. I walked up to Baby Love's door, pressing my ear to it, and heard nothing.

The sobbing started up again, and my attention went right to where I figured it was coming from.

I took careful steps to Leo's room door where the sounds were coming from. I did as I usually did with Baby Love's door, pressing my ear to it.

I heard sniffing, or what sounded like it, behind Leo's closed door. I couldn't be too sure.

But when I turned Leo's doorknob and pushed the door in gently, I confirmed what my ears had already picked up.

As the door opened, I saw him sitting on the floor, his long legs bent at the knees, his forearms balanced on top of them, arms hanging over. His head hung to his chest, his body visually showing what he was feeling inside.

I had never seen Leo break down before. His sobs were quiet at first as I stood at the doorway. It was almost like he was trying to hold them back, a stifled sound that you could mistake for a cough or a clearing of the throat.

I hadn't seen him cry not once. While I was always breaking down for seemingly anything and anywhere, I had never seen Leo shed a tear over losing his best friend. He just always seemed to hold it all together and remain strong for the both of us. But as I stepped closer, I could see the hurt I had been wondering if he ever felt.

I could see the real struggle on his face, the way his jaw clenched tight, fighting against the wave of emotions that finally spilled over.

I whispered, "Leo?"

He gasped, popping his head up, then quickly taking a swipe at his face to clear it of tears.

His eyes. My heart broke when they locked on mine before he forced himself to look away. His eyes that were normally so bright and commanding were dimmed, red-rimmed, and glossy with unshed tears.

"Ivy, man," he expressed, his voice hoarse beyond recognition. "What the fuck? You don't know how to knock?"

His mouth said one thing, but his eyes and his posture said something else. Those eyes were revealing so much behind them.

"This is the second time you just walked up in here without knocking." He turned his back to me, inhaling a deep breath while swiping his hand down his face again.

How could I have been so naive? Believing that we just were grieving differently, but he was clearly hurting.

His reaction said it all for me. I was hearing his words, and he was doing a good job at trying to deflect, but all I could see was hurt.

"Leo," I affirmed this time.

"Nah, man." He shook his head, his back still to me. "Get out."

He was so guarded, but the moment was everything but that. It was a raw, unguarded moment that shattered his usual demeanor of easy confidence and playful charm... something that always annoyed me about him. He was so unserious, taking everything for a joke. He'd been this way for as long as I knew him. I often wondered how he and Tyrell got along because Tyrell was never as playful as Leo.

Leo was inhaling deep breaths, my guess trying to get himself together, and I just wanted to show him he didn't have to. That it was okay to just let that shit out.

So I went to him, my steps along his floor letting him know I was closing the distance between us.

He barely turned to face me when he made a beeline for his bed. "Ivy, go."

He'd plopped down into a seat when I was only steps away. And when I took a seat beside him on his bed, he kissed his teeth and dropped his head back between his shoulders.

"Oh my God," he expressed to the ceiling. "Please, don't do this shit right now."

I didn't say anything else. Didn't think I needed to. The only thing I did was wrap my arms around him and pulled him in. And he collapsed in my arms.

I held him tighter, feeling my own tears wanting to fall too. They welled in my eyes, and I took a couple of deep breaths to keep them inside.

So many times, Leo was my strength. And there was some reassurance with that. That I could break down, and he would be there to make me feel whatever I was feeling would pass soon.

I wanted to be that for him.

But watching him sent a pang in my chest. Several pangs. A deep, aching echo of his pain that made me draw him nearer, doing my very best to offer any comfort I could in that moment.

Aside from his sobs, the night was quiet, and sleep for me was long gone after seeing him like this.

"All this shit, man," he said lowly, pulling away slowly, covering his face with his big hands. "Having to raise a baby..." He dropped his hands to look at me. "Having to live here. Needing to still perform my best at every game. God." Leo inhaled a deep breath. "I'm just tired, Ivy." He shook his head. "I miss my boy." Leo's chin quivered before he balled his lips to force it to stop.

I placed a hand against his back and started running my palm up and down the length of it.

"When the fuck does it get easier?" he asked, turning his attention to me.

His eyes were even more red-rimmed than they were when I walked in here, skin flush. I wasn't sure how long he'd been crying before I walked into his room, but it must have been for a while because he looked terrible... but handsome too.

The vulnerability, the openness. I had never seen Leo express anything emotionally. It's like I said, everything was always a joke to him. Class clown shit 24/7. But that night, his sadness was humanizing, showed emotional depth. His willingness to be vulnerable, even though he tried to fight it at first, reaffirmed that despite our differences, he trusted me, and that did something to me. I almost felt protective watching him like this.

We held our stare for the longest, saying nothing, my hand still caressing his back.

And I'm not sure how it happened, but I went from caressing his back to watching him in real time close the space between us until his lips were pressed up against mine. And while I was there as it was happening, it almost felt like I wasn't. Like I'd stepped out of myself and was watching as our lips parted and our tongues joined in each other's mouths.

I dropped my hand from his back as he wrapped his arm around me to pull me closer, an attempt to bring our kiss deeper. And the moment I realized what was happening, what we were doing, I pulled away, abruptly breaking our kiss.

My hand was at my lips a second later.

"Shit," he whispered, bringing his hand to his mouth to swipe down. "Damn, my bad."

We were quiet for a few breaths. In my head, I was sorting through the thick of the emotions. Trying to wrap my mind around how the hell we'd gotten here.

"I'm not thinking straight," he said. "I'm trippin'. I'm trippin' so hard. I'm sorry."

And maybe he was.

I had to be too because a second later, I was the one closing the space between us now, leaning into him, my face to his, pressing my lips back against his.

He moaned, his arm quickly wrapping around my waist as he not only kissed me back but also reclined us back onto his bed, him taking a position over me.

Lips parted and our tongues reunited after a short separation. And I melted under him, feeling his body pressed against mine as he caressed my tongue with his. His breath against my skin, his pulse beating with mine. It was insane that all of that was capable between us.

Honestly, I was wrecked with so many emotions. Grief, shock, insomnia. So much shit was bombarding my consciousness at one time every day since Kendra and Tyrell's accident, that I just needed something, anything else to feel.

I was desperate for an escape. I needed more than a getaway. I wanted to run away from this supposed new norm neither of us asked for. I needed a heavy dose of anything to forget right now. Something Leo's hands skating up the hem of my shirt to palm my breasts underneath provided.

I remember when Kendra returned to our dorm to let me know the guy she was dating had a friend, and we would double-date that night. Believing that the friend would have to be like her new guy Tyrell, I didn't hesitate to agree to go out with them. Tyrell was responsible, attentive, and of course handsome. His friend had to be all those things too, I thought.

Within seconds of meeting him, I realized I couldn't stand the friend, Leo. He was too goofy, constantly busting jokes, and just annoying.

Years later, he was making my body feel things it hadn't ever felt as he slid a hand into my varsity shorts then behind my panties, his fingers nestling comfortably between my lower lips.

I exhaled into his mouth, spreading my legs wide enough for him to circle those fingers against my wet bud as I circled my hips in time with his caresses.

He moaned against me, growing hard against me too, sending my mind racing with so many thoughts I couldn't single one out to give it the attention it needed.

Because I didn't want to do that shit. I didn't want to think. I wanted to feel any and everything else, remember?

So peeling myself out of my shorts and him ridding himself of his lounge pants was the obvious next move. Getting a condom would have been the other, but we were so caught up, *I* was so caught up in the moment, that reaching between us and angling him against my warmth seemed like the natural next move.

Our eyes locked as he steadied himself so I could guide him in. Our jaws dropping at the same time. At the point of penetration, our pupils dilated.

"Fuuuck," he whispered, sounding defeated, and drawing that word out until he was out of breath. That acted like the relinquishing of common sense for the both of us as he initiated his first series of deep thrusts shortly after that.

We were adults. Friends. Two attractive, consenting adults who were also going through one of the most uniquely traumatizing experiences.

This should be fine. It should be okay... right?

Leo hooked my right thigh with his right forearm, holding me wide open and plunging deeper.

"Shit, you're inside of me," I whispered, too swept up in the moment to grasp the full weight of my words. I struggled to keep my eyes from rolling back, giving in for just a second. "Damn, Leo, you're so deep!"

"I can go deeper," he said to me, his eyes becoming low-lidded the more heat we conjured up between us. "You want me to go deeper, Ivy? Can you take it?"

His question left his lips and got lodged in my consciousness, leaving me stuck between who we were and what we were doing. Him aiming to make me unravel and me desperate to see his face transform with mine from the pleasure happening inside of me.

My walls fluttered uncontrollably, my back arched instinctively, pushing back against him as if possessed, meeting each of his thrusts.

In our stare, I nodded a response to his question, and that made him breathe harder. Go deeper.

I bit my bottom lip in reaction, parting my lips long enough to tell him, "You fuck really well."

"Yes, I do," he said with a smirk, his face contorting briefly as he reacted to my grip. "Only *you* would say something like that out loud."

"Shut up." I whimpered then exhaled. "And you're gonna make me come if you keep doing that, Leo."

"*Mmm-hmm.*" He folded his bottom lip into his mouth. "Why do you think I'm doing it like *that*, Ivy?"

I clenched my teeth, recognizing a familiar pull down low between us.

"'Cause ain't that the point?" He grabbed a handful of my ass and held me open. "For us to come, Ivy League?"

He stared into my eyes and glided in even further.

"Let me see you come for me," Leo murmured, pushing deeper with a grin. "Ivy League," he groaned, his voice thick with desire as he licked his lips. "Still hate that nickname, Ivy, or does it feel different now?"

And for the first time in the history of him teasing me with that annoying ass nickname... I liked it this time. Loved it, actually. Or did I love him sliding in and out between my slick walls, encouraging me to lose myself in the friction.

"Fuck you, Leo," I said or mouthed, I couldn't tell. I couldn't hear my voice or hear anything for that matter, blinking erratically until I couldn't help conceding to the weighted pulsing where we connected. It was so intense I had to close my eyes and brace myself. The sensation swelled like a wave, clouding my eyes and blurring my vision with tears.

"Yeah, just like that," he gritted over me. "God, your pussy feels so good around me. Why do you feel so fucking good?"

And he felt so good inside of me too, but I couldn't respond. Too out of breath to speak, because I was coming and finally feeling good again after months of feeling like shit. My jaw was slacked as my mind was finally cleared of everything. My thoughts, concerns, and doubts. Unable to consider who was making me come and why he probably shouldn't have been the one to have an orgasm with.

That feeling I was desperately chasing, the one beyond the sadness and grief, finally hit me. My toes curled so hard they ached, and my whole body started shaking under Leo, threatening to throw off our rhythm

He grabbed the bars of his headboard, using his grip around it for leverage. He grunted while thrusting harder, going deeper, our bodies slapping against each other now, echoing with our voices around his room.

I clung to him like I had never clung to a man ever in my life. Held him so close I could feel his heart hammering with mine as I journeyed through a pulsing sensation that forced me to forget who he was and who I was to him. It just silenced everything. Those racing thoughts were no more, replaced with ringing in my ears. I felt safe, raw, hollowed out, and like I was falling up and flying at the same damn time.

"Yes, yes," he grunted through bared teeth, pumping his hips back and forth with methodical thrusts, slamming into me at this point as he trembled like crazy against me too. "Fuck, Ivy, fuck, ahhh!"

We shook together, the bed vibrating beneath me as our cries echoed around Leo's room.

"Ahh, ahh, shit," Leo whispered, his jaw slacked, bottom lip quivering as his eyes locked on mine again.

And all I could do was watch without blinking as his entire frame vibrated in my grip while he struggled to pull on air.

At the end of it all, Leo and I collapsed onto the bed, him on top of me. We laid there frozen. Still. Him inside of me, his dick still pulsing between my walls that felt like they were milking him. We tried like hell to catch our breaths. I hadn't let him go, and he hadn't let me go either. Neither one of us wanting to leave the moment.

For me, I refused to let him go, deep down fearing what would happen when we locked eyes for the first time after. Most of all, I feared what would come next after that and what us doing this meant moving forward.

ELEVEN

"IT IS SO beautiful in here, *ugh*!" Vanessa said across from me. "So green." She giggled next.

I forced a smile and nodded. "For real."

She reached across the table, placing a hand atop mine and then closing her hands over it.

"I'm so happy you asked me to come out with you tonight, again," she said with a playful smile. "Three nights in a row, it's like we're reliving our first summer together. I feel like I haven't seen you this much in forever."

I lifted my glass of brandy to my lips to take a sip.

"But I don't hold that against you, so please don't think I do," she added, her eyes softening as she looked at me. "I know you've been through a lot, so I totally understand your absence."

All I could do was nod.

"A whole baby." She cringed, shaking her head. "How are you coping, anyway?"

We were at *Celestine Sky*, a socialite's dream. It was a favorite amongst celebrities too. A fact that played a part in me asking Vanessa to have dinner with me here. I'd been asked for my autograph at least five times since we'd arrived and honestly? I needed that shit. I needed all the distractions and extra interactions. On any other day, it would frustrate me a little, but tonight I needed it more than ever.

Vanessa lifted her menu to her eyes. "What are you thinking about getting?"

When she did that, she moved the air a little in the room, sending the fruity, floral notes of her perfume across the table.

Her perfume was the first thing I noticed when my driver picked her up from her apartment. It made me skip a breath. And it made me skip a breath again sitting across from her.

It was the same perfume Ivy wore. Besides knowing it was the same perfume from scent alone, I knew it was the same because I was the one who bought the fragrance for Vanessa after smelling it on Ivy two summers ago. Big mistake. Because just like earlier, when I got the first whiff of Vanessa's perfume, my mind pulled me back to that night with Ivy in an instant when I smelled it on Vanessa again.

Ivy and I laid there for what felt like forever, long after catching our breath.

Once the moment set in, and the realization that what had happened, had happened, I guess neither one of us wanted to look at each other.

I decided to be the brave one, inhaling a deep breath and pulling away, breaking our connection below the waist.

Ivy let out a soft sigh when I created distance between us. She immedi-ately pulled her legs to herself while tugging at the hem of her oversized tee in an attempt to cover the lower half of her body.

When we finally looked at each other, we just stared. It was so quiet in my room I could hear her heart beating.

My eyes were on fire, burning from lack of sleep, burning from being up at an hour I shouldn't have been, and burning after crying.

I was crying. Thought it was too late to have been heard. All due to a dream I had of Tyrell. He didn't say anything in the dream but looked happy. And I kept telling him how much I missed him, how much life had changed since he'd been gone. The dream didn't last very long, and I felt so fucking incomplete when I got up suddenly from it. Instead of going back to sleep, I was filled with so much emotion I couldn't fight back, and I just broke down, crying on my bedroom floor... until Ivy showed up.

We were staring at each other now. After... everything. All of that. All the sensations, and emotions, and other things I couldn't quite put names to.

"We didn't use a condom," were her first words to me. She said them low, as if she were saying it to herself.

"Are you still on birth control?" I rasped.

She nodded quickly.

"Aight." I swallowed hard. "So, then... we're good... right?"

"Yeah," she whispered.

"I always use a condom," I said, clearing my throat. "This is the first time I didn't, so..."

"Same."

Ivy inhaled an audible breath and was about to say something else when we heard the sharp cries of Baby Love from his nursery. Ivy gasped next. Both of our attention went to my door that was still open.

No doubt all that shit we just did woke him from sleep. I'm pretty sure we woke the whole fucking neighborhood... or what was of it.

"I'll get him," I told her, turning to focus on her again. "I got it."

It was my attempt to get away from her. And I did. After getting dressed and going to the baby's nursery, I gave him his bottle, and he fell asleep while drinking it. I could've returned to my room, but I chose to spend the remainder of the night in the nursery, falling asleep on the rocking chair.

The next day, I had to be in the city for training and spent a little extra time in the gym practicing, too damn concerned about what would happen if I returned to Greene Gardens.

I went on a date with Vanessa that night and was distracted, just like tonight.

I had asked Vanessa out to eat every night after that night with Ivy. It was now the third night after, and I was out with Vanessa again... distracted.

"You think you'll come back to my place tonight?" she asked, running her manicured nails through her short hair while batting her long lashes.

"Damn." I chuckled nervously. "Can we eat first?"

She giggled. "I just thought I'd ask. While I love that we have been going out literally three nights in a row, I would love for you to hang with me at my place after." Her hand was across the table again as she laid it against mine. "I really, really miss you, Leo."

Her touch was missing something.

I appreciated Vanessa's caring nature. She agreed to hang out with me at short notice and with no hesitation. She was always like that. But there was always something about our relationship, if you could call it a relationship, that always seemed like it was missing something. There was always something in all my relationships where I felt like I was missing something.

But that wasn't the case the night Ivy and I hooked up.

Though the situation was so wrong, she felt so right. *We* felt right. I fit inside her like a puzzle piece. Where her hands laid on me just came naturally. Like they were always supposed to be there.

And that finish? I had never experienced a nut like that in my life. It ran through me like electricity, making me feel like I'd been blasted out of this planet for several seconds. It was wild.

I couldn't get it out of my head.

I don't know.

After everything, things were awkward, true. But in the act, while we were doing what we were doing, everything was so damn right. Perfect. Pure. Addictive? Because I'd only done it once, and it didn't even last that long, and already I was feeling a sense of withdrawal.

"Leo," Vanessa said across from me.

I switched my head in her direction. "What's up?"

Her eyes moved to my right before she was pointing that way. "Our server asked what would you like to have for dinner?"

I peeked that way, noticing the woman standing there with her pencil and notepad, wearing a smile and waiting.

"Oh." I sat up. "My bad, I didn't even see you standing there… *ummm…*" I lifted my menu and went with the first thing my eyes fell on. "I'll have the herb-crusted halibut. Thanks."

When our server had finished taking our order, leaving Vanessa and me alone again, she wasted no time asking, "Is everything okay?"

I focused on her.

"I mean…" She held up a hand. "I know that everything isn't okay. I just mean you seem a little out of it."

What I wouldn't have given to be able to talk this out with someone. Tell her what happened with Ivy and how it had my mind so fucked up. Because I thought Ivy was the only woman on this planet I would never sleep with. We were so different, and I highly doubted I was her type. But that night, in its own way, what we did was really beautiful. She looked really fucking beautiful with me inside of her, having the most intense orgasm against me. Time froze for me, and I wanted someone to explain to me what the hell I was feeling. Why I wanted her again. Why I felt the need to avoid Ivy because I wanted her again in the worst way, but I knew that was a foolish thought.

Couldn't tell Vanessa that, though. She most definitely wouldn't be understanding about me fucking another woman, even if Vanessa and I weren't in a relationship. Plus, for the two years I've known Vanessa, she has been convinced that Ivy and I had hooked up in the past or would hook up in the future. Vanessa swore Ivy wanted me but was hiding her desires behind our friendship, which was laughable at best. So there was no way I could tell Vanessa what had me spacing out and constantly being sucked back into my bedroom at 3 a.m., unexpectedly enjoying the best sex I've ever had in my entire fucking life.

"I'm good," I told her, forcing another smile. I'd been doing that every night since I asked her out to eat. Lying. "Just… I got a lot on my mind."

Like how tight Ivy's pussy was around me and how I was pretty sure I would be willing to take my final breath buried inside of her, just like that night.

I cleared my throat and reached for my glass, tossing back the brandy.

I was lifting my hand to signal our server to bring another round when Vanessa reached her hand across the table again.

Her touch was so damn empty, my God.

Not like Ivy's. Her touch—from the innocent caress of my back to the dig of her nails in my back—was otherworldly.

"Come back to my place tonight." Vanessa licked her lips, then drew her bottom lip into her mouth to bite. "I'll take care of you."

So I did. I had my driver bring Vanessa and me to her apartment. She didn't waste much time as soon as we stepped through her door. And I did my best to stay in the moment. Tried to be receptive from the ride over as she kept running her hand up and down my neck, leaning in for a kiss.

Any time before the night with Ivy, all of that would have been enough... or was it? Or was I just settling then, like I was settling now as Vanessa walked me to her couch in her living room?

Her hands were at the back of her dress as she zipped it down, the fabric coming undone around her shoulders and then her waist before it was falling to her feet.

Vanessa was a really beautiful woman. Everything about and around her was beautiful. Her apartment was that of a socialite. Furry this, gold-plated that. She was truly a great woman. Then why was what she was doing tonight not doing anything for me?

She was down on her knees, kissing me through my jeans. I dropped my head back against the neck of her couch, squeezing my eyes closed, trying like hell to ground myself in the moment.

But, fuck! Something was missing.

Vanessa unzipped my fly and pulled out my dick that was still very flaccid.

It was never, *ever* flaccid around her.

"Oh," she commented, lifting her gaze to mine. "It's okay." She nodded next, allowing a sweet smile to pull at her lips. "I got you."

And any other time, that would have sufficed, but tonight I just wasn't feeling it.

"You know what?" I gently took her by her wrists and moved myself out of her reach, standing to my feet. "I'm just gonna head home."

"What?" she asked, taking a seat on the couch, watching as I fixed myself. "Why?"

"I'm not feeling too good," I lied. "I'm not in the right headspace, and that's not fair to you."

"It's fine—"

"It's not, Vanessa," I spoke over her. I closed the space between us, taking a seat on the couch beside her for only a moment. I took her by the chin, caressing her there for a breath before leaning in to leave a kiss against her forehead. "I'll call you."

She sighed, then nodded, pressing a hand to my face. "Okay."

Back in the black car I rented and headed down the I-87 en route to Greene Gardens, alone with my thoughts, all I could think about was Ivy and that night. That was all I could think about these last few days.

What the hell was even that?

I had never seen Ivy in that light before, completely pushed the idea of us to the back of my mind the night we first went out with our friends. Very beautiful, she wasn't my type personality-wise. Uptight, way too particular, and headstrong... with a sex face that was making me hard in the back of that black car from memory alone.

I lowered my attention to my crotch and asked, "Really? Now you wanna firm up?"

"What's that, sir?" my driver asked from the front of the car.

I chuckled, lifting my hand and holding it within sight. "Nothing, Greg. I'm just back here trippin' is all."

He chuckled, removing his eyes off the rearview and focusing on the road up ahead.

Because I *had* to be trippin', wanting to do any of the shit Ivy and I did that night again.

We did need to talk about it, though. Since that night, I have been busy, and so has she, barely seeing each other around the house...

Or were we avoiding each other?

I TOOK a seat at the kitchen table and immediately melted into the chair cushion. And not in a good way. My head was heavy, so were my limbs and my eyes. I lifted the cup of coffee I'd just brewed to my lips, taking a slow sip of the hot caffeine, moaning a little at the bite of heat against my tongue and the instant gratification of tasting the robust, sweet coffee.

It was almost 9 p.m., and I'd officially been up for an entire 24 hours. The night before, Baby Love had very choppy sleep. Teething had hit us unexpectedly and was messing with his sleep pattern. He was officially three months old that day. I thought teething happened when they got older. Baby Love's visiting doctor told me I was correct, but in some cases, some babies start teething at the three-month mark. And God, I wish Baby Love wasn't "some babies."

The night before was a horror show. Me, home alone with a baby that wouldn't settle down and stop crying unless I was holding him. Thankfully, I remembered the teething essentials Baby Love's grandparents provided Leo and me with when we first brought him home from the hospital. The teething essentials were packed in a gift basket with other things we could use now and later. I thought it was a bit much, but that proved to be incorrect.

I'd finally gotten him settled down a few minutes prior. He just kept bringing his little fingers to his gums and biting down whenever he wasn't hollering at the top of his lungs.

I dropped my head into my hand and smoothed my fingers against the inner corners of my eyes.

Even light was too much for me at that hour, which was why I was sitting in the kitchen in the dark. I needed to sit in the dark, as tired as my eyes were.

This was the first moment throughout the day that I had gotten some reprieve. I planned to do some recording earlier today, then decided I'd take care of it tonight after putting Baby Love to sleep, but dammit, I was too tired to lift a camera, much less record a video that would be half as interesting as the one that garnered so much attention previously.

I heard Leo chuckling as he stepped down the stairs behind me.

"Of course, baby," Leo said, his voice growing louder as he drew near to the kitchen. "I should be out there in the next hour."

I turned to look at him just as he stepped into the kitchen, switching on the light.

I cringed, turning away from the overhead light in my seat at the kitchen table to cover my eyes with my fingers.

He laughed before the room lit up, then he quickly stopped, saying into the phone, "I'm about to head out now. I'll call you in the car."

I inhaled a deep breath and let it out really slowly through my nose.

Then there was that. Leo and his bullshit.

We had sex. I could finally allow myself to put a name to what happened that night. You wouldn't even know we had sex the way he's been walking around here, avoiding me.

"I didn't know you were down here," he said low, taking quick steps to the fridge. "I just needed some water."

He smelled good. Looked even better. In all black, his designer wool coat and Chelsea boots already on. No different than the way he was smelling and looking the night before... and the night before that. And the night before that...

Every night since the hookup in his bedroom, Leo had been going out. With Vanessa.

I tucked my lips into my mouth to rub, trying my hardest to get rid of the feeling that thought elicited whenever I thought about him going out with her and what he was doing with her.

I really shouldn't have cared, but somehow I did... now.

"You waiting for a burglar or something?"

I lifted my eyes to him.

"Why were you sitting in the dark?"

"Because I'm tired." I nodded my head, still looking at him. "I've been up for the past 24 hours. How about you?"

He blinked in response.

"You look well-rested." I pressed my lips together. "Jubilant."

He was also different. Leo looked different to me since the hookup in his room. He looked at me differently as well since then.

Unable to maintain eye contact with me for more than a few seconds. Always needing to focus on a distraction to have a reason not to look my way.

I shook my head, moving my attention to the baby monitor he picked up from the city weeks ago. He got it the day after I had to leave Baby Love with him to take a much-needed shower. For a few days after that day, Leo was a present guardian to the baby. Showing up and helping to care for Baby Love. But lately, specifically after our hookup days ago, he'd been distant.

And I couldn't bring myself to ask why. Because I didn't want to hear the truth. Because what happened that night was still something I was processing. Alone.

Leo cleared his throat, gesturing toward the door. "I'm about to head out."

"I heard," I said, snapping my neck in his direction. "Must be nice…"

Leo kissed his teeth.

"… to be able to decide on a whim to drive close to an hour to the city to go eat, drink, and be merry."

"Ivy, don't give me that shit."

I jerked my head back.

"I got games every other day," he started. "Flying out and making sure to fly back the same damn day so you won't be here alone with Baby Love the whole time—"

"And somehow I still feel alone with him, hmph." I feigned shock. "Funny how that is."

He pressed his hand to his chest. "I'm here during the day. I help out."

"For an hour or two," I said. "After that, you're back in your room, sleeping off the drinking and partying from the night prior before you're up again taking your ass back out for another night of drinking and partying." I shook my head. "You're using the city and Vanessa," I gritted out, "as an escape from your responsibilities here."

"When did you start having a problem with how I spend my time, Ivy?"

Since he made me feel heaven on earth while still alive. Very alive.

There hasn't been a minute in any day that I hadn't thought about that night he and I had. It was the most random thing I'd ever done, but the most soul-stirring too. I don't hook up. It has never been my thing. Kendra used to say I was too in my head to do it right, and she wasn't lying.

The one time I tried hooking up with a guy I wasn't dating, before the guy and I could get back to my place and actually do it, I had to change my mind because I kept wondering what would happen after. What we would say to each other? How would I send him home? All the questions living in the moment has no answers for, so I've just understood hooking up as being for everybody else and not me.

But the night Leo and I had sex unexpectedly, everything just flowed. Everything just felt so right, including the act itself. I didn't need to get in the headspace to focus or concentrate. Didn't need to overthink, wondering if he was okay and if I was making him feel as good as he was making me feel. I was just feeling and reacting from that feeling, and it was the most amazing thing.

But he's been a jerk ever since.

"If I were you," Leo said, pulling me back into the kitchen with him. "I would take more advantage of the Simmons' and their offer to watch Baby Love."

I kissed my teeth. "I would never do that. I would never ask them to watch the baby so I could go out and drink and *fuck* in the city."

He scoffed a laugh. "Who said anything about *fucking*?"

I squeezed my eyes closed, pissed at myself for saying the one thing that was really bugging me. Because I knew that's what he had to be doing with Vanessa. That's all they ever did. He's joked about them barely having conversations because they spent most of their time on beds always having sex. So I knew that's what they had to be doing with his frequent visits to the city.

Leo held two hands up in front of himself.

"Look," he said, running a hand down his beard. "You're tired right now and understandably frustrated..."

And confused as to what the hell we are at this point.

"I get it." He nodded. "I'm just saying you can take a break from all this too, Ivy."

I rolled my eyes away from him.

"You can get out there, enjoy the life you thought you were gonna have before all this shit went left."

"I don't want to do what you're doing, Leo." I turned in my seat to face him completely. "I don't want to be a deadbeat, just dropping that baby here, there, and everywhere."

His brows shot up. "A deadbeat." He clenched his jaw next. "You calling me a deadbeat now?"

I just stared at him.

He hollered a laugh. "Wow. And for the fucking record, you wouldn't be dropping him here, there, and everywhere. He'd be going to his grandparents. Grandparents who offered to take him whenever."

"You just don't fucking get it." I shook my head. "Handing the baby off to others isn't a solution to the overall issue here, Leo." I pointed at him next. "We don't even have a name for him yet."

"Here we go with this shit," he expressed lowly.

"It's been three months, and you haven't been around long enough for us to decide what we are going to call him."

"Choose a fucking name then, shit."

"Choose a fucking name," I repeated, scoffing a laugh and looking away before refocusing on him. "The point still remains. You have been going out way too much. You have been clubbing, dining, and whatever the fuck else you're doing when you're not here... you've been doing it too damn much."

"And who the fuck made you the authority on that shit?!" he shouted. "*Hmm*? I ain't married to you. We're not together."

I scoffed.

"I am trying, Ivy," he stressed. "I'm *trying*, aight? I'm trying my best to balance my career, my life, and a life I didn't get to choose. I am *fucking* trying here!"

It started as a sound of the baby stirring in his crib, the sound echoing around the kitchen through the baby monitor. A second later, Baby Love released a sharp cry, which made me close my eyes. It wasn't only his crying that made me close my eyes. It was my attempt to keep the tears in.

My life hadn't felt like my life in three months, and at the rate shit was going, it probably never would. Especially now that I'd slept with Leo, who I always felt was just a friend, but now I couldn't place him.

I kissed my teeth, lifting my mug and bringing it to my lips to take a large gulp, knowing it would be cold by the time I made my way back downstairs to finish it.

As I pressed my hands onto the table to stand, Leo told me, "Nah, I got it."

"It's fine," I spat.

"I said I got it," he replied with a level of bass that made me sit my ass back in my seat.

We stared at each other for a moment, Baby Love crying in the background.

How could this have been the same man that made me feel all the good feelings that were humanly possible to feel at one time? Every time I recalled that night, my mind transported me back to that space and time, me coming beneath him for so long. An orgasm I thought would last forever.

"Just relax," he said softly. "I'll take care of him before I head out."

He was out of the kitchen a second later, making his way up the stairs to Baby Love.

I shook my head to myself, dropping my forehead into my hand next.

Would we ever talk about it? Was it him going out or was it him going out to see Vanessa that bothered me? Why did I care? That night he and I shared should've been nothing, but then again, I don't know how to hook up, so I'm pretty sure I didn't do it right. Because I don't think I should be feeling this way.

I dropped my head back between my shoulders, only lifting it again when I heard Leo's voice through the baby monitor.

"Hey, hey, what's up?" Leo said softly as he entered the room. "*Shh*, you aight, you aight. Come here."

His voice sounded different. Calmer and so damn... sexy.

I brought the monitor closer to me, bringing it closer to my ear.

"Why you in here making all this noise anyway? *Hmm*?"

The tension in my shoulders and chest gradually released as I listened.

It was amazing how quickly Baby Love settled the moment he heard Leo's voice.

"I got you something," Leo said next. "The good stuff too. That liquid gold, homie."

I snickered to myself while shaking my head.

"You know you living the life right?" Leo asked Baby Love next. "You get up whenever you want to, celebrated when you fall asleep, get someone to get you a bottle. Sometimes it's me, often it's that fine ass lady down there giving me hell right now. Man, let me tell you."

I kissed my teeth.

"You are very loved, little guy," he whispered. A second later, there was the sound of him giving Baby Love a kiss. That made me press my hand to my chest. "You still scare me, but... you are very loved."

There was silence after that and only the sounds of Baby Love drawing milk from his bottle, making gratifying baby sounds as Leo fed him. Baby Love's milk-drinking sounds always melted my heart hearing it in real time.

Leo was good with him. It was something I noticed after the night I left Baby Love with him. He just needed to be around more often and not acting like we didn't just inherit an entire baby which, yes, meant our lives, and the lives we knew, had to change.

Leo was right, though. Life wasn't life, and it had become hard without warning, but shit, I was figuring it out, and I couldn't help but feel like I was figuring it out alone.

Especially now with the hookup in the mix causing even more confusion in my headspace.

"Aight," he said low, taking careful steps down the stairs behind me. I glanced over my shoulder to meet his eyes. "He's sleeping again. I fed him, burped him, all that."

I said nothing, just kept looking at him.

He draped a long arm over the staircase's banister. "So, we good now?"

What a loaded-ass question. And good on what exactly?

Not wanting to be the Ivy I knew got under his skin, I nodded.

"*Mm-hmm*," I added.

But could we ever be good again?

"Aight." His back was to me as he pulled open the house door, stepping out. "I'll see y'all in the morning."

Damn.

Just like that.

I rolled my eyes and inhaled a deep breath, my shoulders tensing and my heart too.

Did Leo feel anything the night we were intimate? I know he has a lot of sex. Vanessa was the most serious non-relationship he's ever had. Before her, it was a different girl every other day. Random-ass women he stacked up for one purpose, to fuck, and fuck often. But did he not feel anything with those women? Any of them? Did he not feel anything with me?

I resolved in that moment that those were way too many questions to have without answers. And I'd get them... from Leo.

leo

I LAY IN BED, my eyes focused on the smooth white ceiling overhead. It had to be after midnight because I'd gotten home after ten that night. A game in the city had ended with a win. I was invited out to celebrate with a few of the players on my team, but I just didn't feel like it.

Ivy and I had gone back and forth a few nights ago, which led to her sending me a text suggesting we take shifts caring for Baby Love whenever he woke up during the night.

I inhaled the deepest breath and released it hard through my mouth when I read her text. This was the shit I didn't like about her. Everything had to be so damn particular. Shifts? For what?

But on the other hand, I couldn't blame her as much. Shit had been tense since we hooked up in my room. I still couldn't bring myself to talk to her about it. There were so many factors a conversation about it could affect. Sex is one of those things that will have a woman acting weird, especially with a man like me who's not into all that committed shit. Not right now in my life. Plus, I didn't want to ruin our friendship. She wasn't my best friend, but Ivy was a really good friend. And she was also a woman who likely could get all caught up over a hookup.

I didn't know, though. I barely saw Ivy with other men to gauge how she behaved in relationships, and I never really heard her complain about guys or anything like that. But regardless of what she had or hadn't done, there was just too much uncertainty about her feelings.

I'd hate to approach her and be all like, *Did you feel what I felt that night? The earth move in a way you'd never felt before? A connection that felt deeper than just some dick and pussy stuff?*

Because, shit, I did. And it's been fucking with me since because I have never felt anything like that in my young life.

Baby Love started stirring and slightly whining through the baby monitor on my side table. I peeked over at it, rising from my reclined position, my attention fixed on the device.

My teammate Jaleel suggested Ivy and I get the monitor to keep a closer ear on Baby Love. Said he's had one for all of his children, especially his youngest—a girl who was almost two years old.

I listened in to see if Baby Love would go back to sleep, just as the baby nurse, Marta, had advised months ago. She'd warned against rushing to him at the first sound of noise, saying it would interfere with his ability to self-soothe.

His stirs and whines quickly transitioned to cries, and I was up on my feet a second later.

The fight I had with Ivy in the kitchen a few nights ago was one of the reasons I got out of bed. She'd looked exhausted when I walked in on her there. And I kind of felt bad about getting ready to go out when she revealed she hadn't slept well because of Baby Love's teething.

Kind of. Because the Simmons had given us an open invitation to watch Baby Love whenever we needed, but Ivy was being too prideful to ask for help—another thing I didn't like about her.

I walked out of my room, shutting the door behind me, and made my way to the nursery.

When I got to the doorway, I stopped in my tracks. Ivy was already in the room, leaning over the crib to pick up Baby Love.

"Oh," I said softly, my eyes shifting from her to the baby and back. "Is it not my night?"

She glanced at me, and I had to take a breath.

She was wearing a robe—the same one she had on a month or so ago when I first noticed how beautiful her legs were and how stunning she looked dressed down. Like that night, her hair was out, the ends wisping against her lower back. Her face was fresh and glowing, highlighting her caramel complexion.

"No, it's not your night," she said, turning her focus back to Baby Love and placing him over her shoulder to pat his back. "Yours is tomorrow."

I nodded, unable to think of anything to say. Her natural beauty left me speechless in that instant. So, I decided to simply turn and leave.

"You can stay," she said to my back, stopping me mid-step. "He needs a change and a bottle, and I forgot to leave a bottle in here."

"Aight," I said to the hallway. "I got it."

Part of why I'd been steering clear of Ivy was because I couldn't pin down her real deal—she's usually all locked up, tough to crack. But that night we hooked up, man, she was all out there—stripped back, wide open, just pure and raw. I was talking my shit until I saw her come undone. Honestly, watching it was just... one of the greatest things I've ever witnessed. She was a whole vision, caught up and letting go, just for me.

And while I'd enjoyed myself and felt something bigger than a meaningless hookup, I wasn't sure if Ivy felt the same. A part of me didn't want to know what rejection would feel like or what it'd mean if the feelings weren't mutual.

There, I said it.

I was down in the kitchen, mixing the bottle, and walking it back up to the nursery in no time.

Ivy stood at the baby's changing table, moving like a pro as she removed one thing and wiped another. I knew she'd get the hang of all this before me. There wasn't anything—whether brand new or something everyone else found hard to do—that she couldn't figure out and master quickly. She was always 100% focused on whatever she was doing. Super detailed, which I just couldn't relate to.

"Can you pass me another diaper?"

Her voice was steady, with no emotion I could pick up on. She spoke to me the way she always did, and honestly, it was kind of relieving. I really wanted to preserve our thing. Life had already turned everything upside down for both of us, but mostly for her.

She was on leave from the network she worked at, choosing to step back so she could figure out how to care for Baby Love. She didn't want her career ambitions to get in the way of everything. Our lives were already unique enough.

So, not discussing the hookup and simply pretending it never happened felt like the best decision in my eyes.

After changing Baby Love, I reached for him, lifting him into my arms and holding him in the way Marta, his baby nurse, taught me. The position allowed him to drink his milk while minimizing the gas he'd have later.

As I fed him, Ivy moved around the room, picking up a few items scattered on the floor. She left for a moment and returned with a newly filled bottle, placing it in the warmer on his baby table for the next feeding.

I tracked her with my eyes as she moved, curious if her thoughts mirrored mine.

When Baby Love fell asleep during his bottle, Ivy draped a burp cloth over my shoulder. Her hand brushed against my neck, sending an instant jolt through my body. The simple touch ignited memories of her hands against me, holding tight while her body responded to everything I gave her that night.

I cleared my throat, adjusting Baby Love's position as I patted his back until he gave me the satisfying burp I was working for.

"Thanks," I said, meeting her eyes.

A small smile started to pull at her lips. I could see it trying to take shape, but she stopped it. "You're welcome."

Baby Love burped again, then nestled into me as I held him for a few more minutes, ensuring he was fully asleep before laying him down in his bassinet. Ivy leaned in, positioning his head carefully so he'd be comfortable.

Once we were sure he was settled, she and I stepped out of the nursery one at a time, her first.

I was closing the door behind us when she said, "Leo."

I turned to face her in the dimly lit hallway. Her eyes sparkled, the natural glow of her cheeks catching the light effortlessly and drawing my attention.

She ran a hand through her hair when she noticed me staring. The movement shifted her robe, hinting at the fact that she wasn't wearing anything underneath.

She focused back on me, licking her lips slowly. "You know we need to talk, right?"

Her voice wasn't her usual *we-need-to-talk* tone, the one full of irritation or exhaustion. This time, it was heavy with something else. Something familiar. Something I'd convinced myself I wouldn't pursue after that night.

But now, standing here, looking at her—beautiful as ever—all that resolve evaporated.

I closed the space between us in one swift move, watching her eyes widen when I slid my hand past her jaw and into her hair. The moment my lips pressed against hers, those same eyes closed.

I half-expected her to push me away. Maybe even slap me for daring to kiss her after how strained things had been. But she didn't. She kissed me back just as fiercely, melting into me and eliminating any remaining distance between us.

Ivy was a phenomenal kisser. She understood the give-and-take, how to submit without losing control, and how to take charge when the moment called for it.

Her soft moan was all the encouragement I needed. I wrapped my arms around her, lifting her by her thighs. All my previous thoughts about why this was a bad idea, why we shouldn't hook up again, or why I wanted to pretend it never happened, vanished.

We went from the hallway to my bedroom, shedding what little clothing we had along the way. By the time she straddled me, one leg on either side, I was already guiding her down onto me.

Greene Gardens had more streetlamps than necessary, illuminating our neighborhood with a steady glow. While we didn't have many neighbors and nothing much to worry about, the streetlights made it unnecessary to use our house lights at night.

That soft glow spilled into my bedroom, casting a warm light over Ivy.

She found her rhythm quickly, rocking and rolling her hips with the confidence of a seasoned rider.

"Shit, woman," I groaned, pushing my head back into the pillow and gripping her ass. "Why is your pussy so fucking tight like this? My God."

I closed my eyes, letting myself drift into the thoughtless bliss she created. My hands slid from her waist to her lower back as I followed her rhythm, each glide pulling me deeper into her.

I bit my bottom lip, completely immersed in the moment, not caring about the fight we'd had days ago or what might come after this.

Just... reckless as fuck.

I opened my eyes to find hers already locked on mine.

That look. The focused, detailed-oriented woman I knew was still there, working in perfect harmony with the spell we'd cast over each other.

She was breathtaking like this. Eyes half-lidded, her skin glowing with sweat, her long hair cascading over her face, covering one of her breasts.

I took her firmly by the waist, my other hand sliding up past her jaw and burying itself in her hair, holding her steady.

"Don't rush it," I breathed, pumping my hips upward deliberately.

Her brows furrowed slightly, her voice trembling as she whispered, "What?"

Her moans began to align with my deliberate, deep thrusts as I slowed my pace even further.

"I wanna take my time this time," I confessed, my eyes locked on hers.

She blinked rapidly, her breath hitching. "What?" she asked again, voice weaker now. "Why?"

"'Cause," I groaned at her slick grip around me. "You feel like a never-ending weekend."

Her lips pressed together, then parted as her eyes fluttered closed, overwhelmed by the sensation. She braced one hand on my chest, her rhythm faltering as I held her in place, controlling every movement.

In that moment, all I wanted was to feel her. All of her. To make this moment last longer than the last. Because even though I had no idea what any of this meant for us, I wanted to remember it, in case this was the last time.

My measured strokes disrupted her rhythm, leaving her gasping and chasing the sensation with desperation. Watching her come undone—her eyes fighting to stay open, her lips trembling—spurred me to shift positions.

I lifted her thigh to assist in turning her onto her back. Slowly, I slid out of her, kissing my way down her body until I nestled my lips between her thighs. Without hesitation, I licked along her folds, flicking my tongue over her sensitive bud.

"Leo," she whispered, my name falling from her lips like a prayer. Her back arched, and her hands gripped the back of my head, keeping me exactly where she wanted me. I stayed there, savoring the way her thighs trembled around my face, listening to her soft gasps and moans as she unraveled.

Her taste lingered on my tongue as I kissed my way back up her body. I positioned myself over her again, meeting her gaze as I guided myself back inside her, slower than ever. I watched as her body stiffened beneath me, adjusting to me tunneling into her, and I couldn't take my eyes off her.

Ivy clung to both ends of the pillow beneath her head, her legs spread wide for me. The sight of her—slick, trembling, her body reacting to every thrust—was hypnotizing. I glanced down to where our bodies joined, mesmerized by the way I disappeared inside her, again and again.

When her eyes slipped shut, I pressed my palm gently to her cheek. "Nah, look at me," I whispered.

Her eyes opened slowly, lids heavy, as I ran my thumb along her bottom lip and let it linger there.

I moved at an agonizingly slow pace, savoring every moment, every sound, every sensation. This wasn't my usual approach—quick, rough, often impersonal—but with Ivy, I wanted time to stop.

We locked eyes, our moans perfectly in sync. Her chest rose and fell faster with each thrust, her lips trembling as her bottom lip quivered uncontrollably.

"Leo," she whispered, her voice filled with something I couldn't quite place.

"What's up, gorgeous?" I whispered back. "I'm listening."

She sucked in a shaky breath, her words halting. "We shouldn't be doing this. 'Cause what are we doing?"

"Feeling really fucking good, for a little bit," I answered truthfully, my voice low and ragged. "Just for a little."

She shook her head slightly, biting her lip as if to hold something back.

"What? Am I not making you feel good, Ivy?" I asked, my thrusts intentional and measured. "'Cause you're making me feel incredible. Are you not feeling what I'm feeling?"

"I am."

"And am I hitting your spot?"

She nodded slowly, her voice barely audible. "You're hitting it like you know it all too well."

The confession sent a shiver through me, and I had to draw in a deep breath to keep my pace steady. "That's all I need to hear right now," I whispered. "Does that work for you?"

Her answer came in a soft, drawn-out moan. "Oooh, yessss."

She looked ethereal in that moment—her eyes blinking rapidly before rolling back, her body tensing, her walls tightening around me. Her release came like a wave, her grip on the pillow, gradually slackening as her body surrendered completely.

The sight and feel of her coming pushed me to my limit. I hooked my forearm behind her knee, shifting my angle as I began thrusting with more urgency. My body moved instinctively, taking over as I lost myself in the moment.

She clung to my back next, her nails digging into my lower back, her breathless cries filling the room.

"Oh my God," she moaned, her voice breaking. "Fuck, Leo. Fuck!"

"Fuck," I echoed, groaning uncontrollably. My voice trembled as I buried myself deeper, holding that position. My body shuddering like crazy.

I collapsed onto her, both of us utterly spent. Our bodies stayed joined, neither of us moving, our breaths mingling in the quiet aftermath.

And just like last time, we didn't say a word.

Shit.

And much like the last time, I found myself hoping we wouldn't say anything about this time either.

FOURTEEN

"HEY, IVY."

"Hey, Mommy," I replied. "What's up?"

Yes, I still called my mother *Mommy*, something my girl Kendra used to tease me about all the time. To me, I was going to be a big kid indefinitely, so calling my mother the name I've been using since I learned to speak came naturally.

"How are you?" she asked on the other end of the line.

I was in my bedroom in Greene Gardens, my eyes fixed on the ceiling, my mind somewhere in outer space.

"Positive answer?" I asked. "Grateful for life. Honest answer? Hanging on by a frayed thread that's about two seconds from popping."

These past few days had been unnecessarily stressful.

"The baby, again?"

"Hmph," I huffed. "Believe it or not, that's the easiest thing I'm dealing with these days."

There was silence for a moment before she asked, "Are you gonna tell me what's troubling you?"

I sighed, squeezing my eyes shut. "It's not something I'm comfortable sharing."

Because how do you broach the subject of hooking up with a friend when you should be focused on taking care of a baby... a baby you never asked for?

I grunted, turning over and pressing my face into my pillow.

"God doesn't give us anything we can't handle," she said over speaker. "You know that, right, Ivy?"

"I know, Mommy," I mumbled into the pillow.

"So, while you may think what you're dealing with—whatever you're dealing with—is too much, it's exactly what is needed to bring you closer to Him."

My mother was a very religious woman. Yet another reason I didn't want to share what was really on my mind.

Leo. Sex with Leo, specifically.

"Anyway," she added, "I just called to check in on you. You know my door is always open, and I haven't seen you since you moved out there. So stop by sometime, please."

I nodded against my pillow, turning my head just in time to say, "I will. Thanks for calling, Mommy."

I ended the call and inhaled a deep, encouraging breath before pushing myself into a seated position and stepping off the bed.

I hated feeling like this, and I was about to do something about it...

At least, I hoped I was about to do something about it.

The hour had just switched to 10 p.m., according to my nightstand clock, as I opened my bedroom door and stepped out. To say these last few days had been one of the hardest and most confusing times would be an understatement.

And while it wasn't directly about Baby Love, it had everything to do with him too.

I inhaled deeply, my steps light as I headed down the hall toward Leo's room—the scene of a crime that had happened twice and had yet to be addressed.

This man had been keeping his distance since that night. Again.

Granted, he'd had games and even an away game the day after

our second hookup. But he didn't bother to call me while he was away.

The whole thing was perplexing. For one, like I said, I don't *hook up*. I don't have sex with people I'm not in a relationship with, so I don't know what or how I'm supposed to feel after. Not that it was his responsibility to coach me through my headspace, but damn— what the fuck was this?

After our second time, he got up and out of bed so fast, I barely had time to process what had just happened. He left the room without a word, went straight to the bathroom to shower, and didn't say anything afterward.

Had plenty to say during sex but nothing after. It was bizarre, and I was over it.

I stopped in front of Baby Love's nursery, peeking through the gap in the door to see him sound asleep. He'd returned to his usual schedule of sleeping through the night, thank God. His doctor explained that disruptions like this were normal—part of the growth process and meeting milestones. Wonder weeks, growth spurts, *blah blah blah*. Honestly, I was so inundated with all things baby, I felt like my brain might explode.

And again, I felt like I was doing it all alone.

I was done with that too.

I needed clarity. I needed the air cleared. Most of all, I desperately needed to understand where Leo and I stood. Because this shit? Hooking up and then him acting like I was some random woman he met at the club didn't feel right.

I needed answers because beyond my hurt feelings—which were definitely bruised at this point—our living situation was at risk. Our co-parenting responsibilities were tied up in whatever this *thing* between us was, and it couldn't go unaddressed any longer.

Most of all, I was tired of feeling like an afterthought. Every time it happened, it was *him* initiating. And every time afterward, it was *me* left picking up the pieces of my emotions.

I stopped in front of Leo's door.

I didn't hesitate or delay. I turned the knob and walked in.

The door opened to him standing in front of his full-length mirror, buttoning one of the final buttons beneath his neck.

As soon as he saw me standing in the doorway, he kissed his teeth, then turned his attention back to his reflection. I heard him inhale a calming breath and exhale it through his lips, shaking his head while keeping his eyes on the mirror.

"How many times I gotta tell you to knock?"

I ignored the question. At this point, I didn't think knocking was important. The man had parts of himself in me so fucking deep, knocking was pointless to me.

"Leo, we need to talk," I said instead, stepping fully inside and closing the door behind me.

He ran his hands down his shirt once he was done buttoning, the sound louder than usual, his frustration evident.

"What's going on between us?"

"Nothing," he replied, quick as hell.

"Nothing?"

He squeezed his eyes shut, peeking down at himself.

Leo looked good. He always looked good. Fashion—while he'd never admit it—was his ministry. Always dressed to impress, his style effortless, and lately, it had been having an effect on me that it had never had before. Not until we started having sex.

"Look," I started, stepping closer. "You know I don't do this."

"Do what?" he asked, finally meeting my eyes.

"Have random ass sex with men who aren't my man."

He turned his head slightly to look at me, his brows pulling together.

"But I've had random sex with you." I pointed at him, trying to keep my voice steady. "Not once, but twice. And after each time, I've wondered what us doing that meant for the long term."

"You're too much in your head," he offered, turning to grab his coat from the armchair in his room. "It's sex, Ivy. Just sex."

My brows shot up.

"Nothing too serious, aight?" He chuckled nervously.

"Nothing too serious, but your ass has been avoiding me every time after?" I folded my arms over my chest. "Explain that to me."

"Avoiding you?" He scoffed, laughing in disbelief. Still, his eyes wouldn't meet mine. Instead, they focused on his coat in his hands and the Chelsea boots on his feet. "I've been traveling for away games or needing to go in for practice. I've been busy, not avoiding you."

"*Mm-hmm*." I pressed my tongue against the inside of my cheek. "So that's why you're struggling to meet my eyes right now?"

He blinked at the floor a couple of times, his lips tucking into his mouth.

"Leo, what is *happening*?" I asked, my voice unrecognizable to me. That question came out as a stuttered whisper. Because as I asked it, I could feel my heart begin to ache. "What's going on right now?"

He swallowed hard, his gaze still glued to the floor.

"Before all this, we were friends," I said. "Maybe not the best of friends, but shit, we had a friendship. But now..." I squeezed my eyes shut, shaking my head. "We are not *us* right now, and I need to know what we are."

He shook his head, rubbing a hand along the back of his neck.

"You say it was just sex, but it didn't feel like that, Leo."

He pressed his lips together and closed his eyes, briefly letting his head drop back between his shoulders.

"I've had sex, and it's never felt like that," I admitted. "And even though sex with people I'm not with hasn't happened before you and me, I don't think it's supposed to feel like this after."

"Ivy—"

"Because how can I feel really good while I'm doing that with you, but really horrible when we're done?"

"Listen." He shook his head, scratching the back of it. "I can't do this with you right now. I don't do this emotional shit..." He took a sharp breath. "I got somewhere I gotta be."

"So, you didn't feel anything?" I asked, my voice lowering even further. A part of me didn't want to hear the truth, but another part of me needed it.

"The two times we were together... you didn't feel anything deeper than just sex, Leo?"

"It was just a moment of weakness, aight?" he said over me, his chest rising and falling rapidly. "It... it didn't mean anything of significance for me."

I jerked my head back. "Wow."

"I'm not saying that to hurt your feelings, Ivy," he said quickly, his tone defensive. "I'm just keeping it real. You know me. You of all people know *me*."

I shook my head slowly, my eyes still stuck on him.

"I'm late," he said, gesturing at his door behind me. "I gotta get going."

"Rushing out but didn't want to rush the other night."

His eyes locked on mine.

My eyes were watering, and I was trying like hell to keep the tears in, but it's like I said—I don't hook up. So of course, I would fucking cry over this.

God!

Leo took one look at me, and his chest seemed to cave in.

"Fuck," he whispered. "Ivy, please don't fucking cry right now, man. Not over this shit."

"If it was just sex," I whispered. "Why did you want it to last?"

It was so quiet after I asked my question.

"If it didn't mean anything of significance, why did you want to take your time?"

"'Cause you felt good, Ivy. Okay?" He closed his eyes briefly, exhaling sharply. "Really good. But that's all that it was. Good sex. Nothing more. Nothing less. Please, just..."

I stared at him, feeling my heart crack.

"We were adults who got carried away... twice," he added. "Adults doing adult things. That's it."

"That's it?" I questioned, my eyes darting across his face.

He looked away.

"Because, Leo—"

"Let's just... focus on Baby Love, like we've been doing," he spoke over me. "Like you said we should."

I closed my mouth in reaction, stunned silent.

"Let's not complicate things any further with this, aight?"

I released a scoffing laugh, quickly drying my eyes while sniffing back the ones that wanted to fall.

He sighed, closing the distance between us.

"No." I shook my head, stepping back from him. "Just fucking go."

"Ivy—"

"You know what?" I turned to snatch open his door. "I'll go."

"Ivy, wait," he said behind me as I took large steps back to my room. "Hold on a second."

But before he could add anything more, I was in my room, slamming my door and locking it. I pressed my back to the door, slapped my hand to my mouth, and held back as much sound from my crying as I could.

"Ivy," Leo said on the other side of my door, knocking softly. "Come on, open the door."

I shook my head, doing my best to quietly suck back my cries, keeping my hand firmly against my mouth.

"Ivy, open the door," he said softly, his voice sounding like he was flush against the surface. "Please."

I inhaled a deep breath and pushed myself off the door. Instead of opening it, I walked away, heading to my bathroom and closing that door too.

There was nothing left to say. He made it very clear. And if he were feeling something but simply didn't want to say it, I didn't like that shit either.

I turned on my shower and peeled off my clothes, praying that the water would cleanse my skin—and the feelings I thought were developing for Leo—but that I needed to just go away.

And fast.

leo

THE SOUND of my mother moving pots along a burner grate as she rambled on about how she wasn't expecting me but was so happy to see me filled my sound-space.

"Thankfully, I stopped at the market earlier," she said, her eyes searching her counter. "Because I got some stuff here to make your favorite. You're hungry, right?"

All I did was nod before leaning forward over the island, folding my arms so I could balance my chin on top of them.

My mother turned to glance at me before turning completely to face me, waving her wooden spoon at me.

"Aht, aht," she said with a grin. "You know the rules. You wanna eat, you better help. Up, up!"

I snorted a laugh, standing from my seat and making my way around it toward the stove.

My visit to my mother's house was not planned, but I couldn't take staying in Greene Gardens for another minute. My team and I had a couple of rest days between games, which would've been great before all this shit with Ivy—but now it just made my time at Greene Gardens feel like torment.

I bought this house for my mother. It took a lot of convincing for her to move out of our old one, with her fussing that the old house was her forever home.

But eight years ago, when I was drafted by the Ballers and received my sign-on bonus, one of the first things I knew I wanted to do was buy my mother a bigger house.

She worked hard raising me on her own. I didn't make life as easy as I could've growing up. It was her who put me in sports at a young age. I did so many sports, and I finally settled on basketball, which became more than a way to keep me out of trouble when school was out. It became my ticket to college and, eventually, a professional basketball career with the Ballers at twenty-two. I was eight years strong with my team. And that was all my mama.

"How are you feeling?" she asked, her attention down on the green peppers. "You look... tired."

I sighed and shook my head at the same time. "It's a lot of stuff happening right now, Mama," I confessed. "Too much."

She stared at me for a moment, her eyes scanning my face.

I snorted to myself. Ivy did the same thing a lot, and it always reminded me of my mother. It was probably why I hated when Ivy did it.

"Get the tomatoes from the fridge so you can cut them up," she instructed, gesturing that way. "And tell me what's going on."

My mother's house was every bit her style—from the soft pastel blue paint on just about all the walls to the flower baskets that hung on the spacious wrap-around porch, it was all Cheryl Vanguard.

My father, Felix Vanguard, died when I was only a kid, two months after my eighth birthday. I have memories of him, but none concrete enough. My mother and he were not on the greatest of terms when she finally got pregnant with me, and once I was born, my arrival seemed to worsen what was already turning sour in their marriage. She doesn't speak of it often, even at my big age. She always says she wants me to maintain a good memory of him because, at the end, that was all that mattered.

She always said I was a lot like him… and not always in a good way.

"Ivy and I," I started. "We got beef."

My mother turned her head to look my way. "What did you do?"

I barked a laugh. "Damn. Why *I* had to have done something?"

"Because Ivy is a sweet woman who don't look like she causes problems."

I shook my head as I reached for the knife to begin dicing the tomatoes I'd gotten from the fridge. "That's foul, Mama."

"Well…" She turned to look at me. "Is it true?"

I stopped dicing to drop my head and inhale a deep breath.

"Because the last time I spoke with you about this, I told you not to leave everything up to her," she started. "Raising a baby is difficult. Then you tack on the fact that neither of you were ready for that. She can't do it alone."

"And that's what I've been trying to tell her," I said. "The Simmons have offered to take the baby many times to give us a break. But Ivy's all, *I don't want to just drop our responsibilities on them. And blah, blah, blah.*"

"Why would she say that?"

"*Hmm?*"

"*Hmm?*" my mother mocked. "Why would she feel that having the Simmons take the baby would be like dropping responsibilities?"

"Because…" I dragged out. "She feels I go out too much and I'm barely in Greene Gardens helping out."

My mother pointed her knife at me. "And there it is."

"Mama, I gotta go out to not only make club appearances but to destress," I insisted. "I'm trying to get to the championships. I gotta make money. I didn't plan for any of this. I wasn't ready."

"All I'm hearing is 'I, I, I,'" my mother interjected. "What about her? She wasn't ready either. And considering how driven that girl is, I'm sure she has her own career goals and plans."

I looked off.

"And I'm sure she likes to have a little fun of her own too and wouldn't want to be cooped up in a house raising a baby she wasn't ready to raise either."

I mumbled, "Ivy boring as hell, so I highly doubt the fun part."

My mother was quick to pop me up the side of my head as soon as all the words came out of my mouth.

"*Ow*, damn!" I shouted, grabbing my head. "Why'd you do that?"

"Because you're being selfish," she said. "That's why."

I kissed my teeth.

"So is that why y'all are beefing?" she probed. "Because you keep leaving the house to party?"

"*Umm*, yes and no."

She stared at me for a moment.

I squeezed my eyes closed and kept them shut when I confessed, "We slept together."

My mother's jaw dropped. "Oh, my God."

"Mama, please."

"Leo," she said, her voice heavy with disappointment—which was exactly why I didn't want to tell her anything.

My mother has been on me for the longest about my sleeping around with different women. She was proud of me for sticking with Vanessa this long, but she kept asking when I was going to take the relationship to the next level. I never revealed that I had no plans to, because we didn't even have a real relationship, and I was content with that. But now, me telling her I had sex with Ivy? Yeah, she wasn't going to go easy on me.

"I skipped a date for her," I confessed. "I had plans to go out the last time Ivy and I had an argument, and I skipped my date for her."

"Why?"

I stared at her for a moment and then said, "You can't get mad."

Her shoulders slumped. "Leo, what did you do?"

"I... I made her cry."

My mother gasped, lifting her hand again to hit me upside the head, but I stepped back.

"Now you about to piss me off!" she shouted.

"It wasn't on purpose," I said. "I just..." I dropped my head and inhaled a breath, pinching the inner corners of my eyes.

"You just what?"

"I don't want to hurt her or break her heart because of my own hangups over commitment. And Ivy's the type to want shit— I mean, stuff like that—and I just, I'm not for that."

"But you're fine with sleeping with that girl and then, from what it sounds like, acting like a damn jerk afterward," she snapped, sucking her teeth. "Dammit, Leo, I didn't raise you to behave like this."

"I know."

"You have to fix it."

"I am." I nodded. "That's why I told her I would move out."

"You told her what?!"

I'd knocked on Ivy's door, waiting for a response. I hadn't seen her since the night before when she left my room and entered hers, locking her door.

I felt terrible after seeing those tears slide from her eyes.

Terrible enough to call Vanessa and let her know I couldn't make it out to Manhattan. I'd tried at least five times that night to get Ivy to open her door. Knocking, then resorting to sitting outside of it with my back to the door. But she never opened the door.

After sitting outside her door for an hour, I returned to my room, changed out of my clothes and into something comfortable, and spent the rest of the night in Baby Love's nursery, watching him sleep.

I never thought it would be possible to find comfort around him, but there was something about him that made me feel right. Good.

I cared for the baby and wanted the best for him. He deserved to grow up in an environment his parents would have created for him—calm, serene, healthy. This shit with Ivy and me was simply not heading in that direction. Not after our back and forth.

"Come in," Ivy said when I knocked again.

I turned the knob and stepped in, finding her at her work desk, setting up her tripod.

Since becoming a guardian, she hadn't gone into the city for work. They'd offered her a column, and she'd been uploading sports commentary to her YouTube channel, which had been growing. She was finding her way in this situation we didn't expect to find ourselves in with Baby Love, and it was really inspiring.

I didn't want to be the person to ruin the new life she was building.

"How are you?" I asked, closing her room door.

She peeked over at me before turning her attention back to what she was doing. "What do you want, Leo?"

She was dressed down, a look she's become accustomed to since moving to Greene Gardens. Before moving here and having to care for a baby, Ivy used to be glammed up 24 hours a day. Hair smoothed to the top of her head, face covered in the most expensive foundation and lipstick money could buy. Clothing always perfect. But lately, her hair had been up in messy buns, her attire simple tees over leggings that, even though covered her up, showed off the beautiful shape of her legs.

That was the thing—to me, Ivy had been her most beautiful since living out here. She was perfect before moving out here, but these days, she was absolutely ethereal to me. And I didn't want the stress between us to change her any further, or for the worse.

"I'm gonna move out."

Her hand stopped twisting the bottom piece of the tripod for a beat before she was back at it.

"Things are clearly getting weird between us." I cleared my throat. "And I feel like shit for making you cry last night."

She shook her head, her attention still not on me.

"We can speak with the estate lawyer and see how we can split guardianship while living in separate locations."

From the side, I could see her balling her lips then releasing them to tuck into her mouth.

"I just feel like maybe we need some space between us—"

"Whatever, Leo," she said, turning to look at me, her eyes slightly red-rimmed. "Sure." She nodded. "Moving out sounds like the best thing right now. So, let's do it. Can you leave now?"

"Dammit, Leo," my mother said, shaking her head really slowly.

I ran a hand down my face.

"You act like you have no self-control," she said, placing her knife on the counter. "You couldn't have just co-parented with Ivy and not slept with her?"

"I didn't intend to."

"Oh, so did she trip and fall on your—"

"Mama, please," I interjected, holding out a hand. "Please don't finish your question."

"I'm just really trying to wrap my mind around why you would complicate things with meaningless sex when you two have a *huge* responsibility now that depends on you working as a team. Why would you do such a foolish thing without considering the consequences of your actions?"

"It wasn't meaningless, though," I said low. "I really wish it were because maybe if it were meaningless, I wouldn't feel this damn conflicted."

My mother jerked her head back. "What? What do you mean?"

I exhaled all the air in me through my mouth. "I felt something different with her that I've never felt with any other woman. I don't know what it was because I'm not familiar with it, but it felt... different."

My mother left the counter altogether, reaching for the island stool. "Child, I need to sit."

I dropped my head to scratch the back of it.

"So, what are you saying, Leo?"

I shook my head. "I don't know."

"Do you..." She lowered her chin to look at me under her lashes. "...love her?"

"I don't know." I met her eyes. "Maybe?"

My mother's hand was at her mouth. "Oh my God, Leo."

I released a stuttered exhale as soon as I said the words.

Because maybe I did love Ivy. And although I've had love for her as a friend, this just felt different.

"Okay, then, tell her," my mother said next, gesturing with her hands. "Go home and tell her how you feel. Don't avoid talking about it by moving out, thinking that's a solution."

"Nah." I shook my head. "We can't."

"Why not?"

"Because doing something like that, giving in to something like that, would change the relationship and possibly ruin our friendship and the co-parenting we have to do for the baby. And I just... I know I'mma fuck it up, Mama."

She pointed at me. "First, watch your mouth."

I snorted a laugh. "My bad."

"Second, have more faith in yourself, Leo." She nodded. "Be more confident with this. Why on earth would you mess things up?"

"Because that's what I do, and that's why I don't do relation-ships." I shrugged. "I don't have them, and I don't want them. I don't like the restrictions they place on me, and I don't like putting those restrictions on the women I deal with. I do me, and I want them to do them."

"So you'd be okay with Ivy doing what y'all did with someone else?"

"Hell no," I was quick to reply. "And... that's the other reason I just know we can't do this."

My mother sighed.

"One bad argument, one weird-ass suspicion." I shook my head. "It could end everything. And we got this baby now..."

"Well, look." My mother stood from her seat and returned to her place at the counter where she'd been cutting peppers. "Avoiding the conversation you two need to have, discussing the truth about your feelings and possibly hers? Could lead to more regret than being brave enough to face what you two discussing this will mean. You're telling me letting fear take the wheel is the move over gaining love and the fulfillment that may await with it?"

"I'm saying I didn't sign up for none of this, damn," I said, running my hands down my face. "I didn't sign up to lose a friend, didn't sign up to become a guardian to his baby, damn sure didn't sign up to fall for Ivy, 'cause shit, what planet am I on that this is happening?"

She pointed at me again, and I threw my hands up.

"My bad for cussing."

My mother's attention returned to the cutting board.

"Too much is changing and too fast, Mama."

"I know," she said. "But God doesn't make mistakes. God doesn't give us things we cant handle. God gives us the things that will strengthen those traits of excellence that we don't think we have but have been there all along. We just gotta be brave enough to uncover them. You're blocking your blessing."

"What?"

She turned to look at me and repeated, "You are blocking your blessing. You thought that you were going to live the life *you* thought you wanted, but God is giving you what God wants for you, and you're blocking it. Stop being foolish and a scaredy cat, and accept it."

I knew Ivy and I would need to clear the air; there was no way around that. I just didn't know how, especially when the last time I tried to talk to her, she wouldn't even look me in the eyes except to tell me to leave her alone.

I feared I'd fucked things up too much now. But I wouldn't count myself out just yet. Whatever I decided to do, it would either mend our friendship or fracture that shit even further.

* * *

Honking horns and the sound of cars rolling along the asphalt outside my loft kept drawing my attention.

I was back home at a place I thought was home. It wasn't Greene Gardens. There were sounds here—city sounds. Cars, horns, and people talking loudly on their phones. All the things I swore I missed while trying to create a life in Greene Gardens, but in that moment, the reality wasn't as satisfying as I thought it would be.

I hadn't officially moved out of the house Ivy and I shared with Baby Love. After my conversation with my mother, I'd returned to Greene Gardens, sure I could work things out, but Ivy had been distant. For two days, she barely said a word to me unless it was about Baby Love.

She was done. I couldn't really blame her.

To keep things from getting too awkward, I packed up a week's worth of the things I'd moved into Greene Gardens and brought them back to my loft in the city.

I'd been invited to a few events and asked to make some club appearances during the week I'd been back, but I just wasn't feeling it.

The crazy part? My loft always felt like home. But now, it didn't.

All the lights in the place were off. The only glow came from the TV screen in front of me.

It felt so empty compared to the constant activity at the house upstate. There, I could always count on Baby Love's cries filling the air or the sound of Ivy's furry slippers brushing against the carpet outside my door, moving like she was sweeping the floor with her feet.

I snorted at the thought. That sound used to annoy me—hearing her shuffle to Baby Love's nursery—but now? I missed it.

I let out a deep breath and forced myself to focus on the TV. I had all these streaming services and couldn't find a damn thing to watch.

It was after midnight. I could've been out, making money and getting free drinks at a club appearance, but the thought of it didn't appeal tonight.

Realizing I'd been scrolling through streaming apps for far too long, I turned off the TV and grabbed my phone.

I opened social media and started scrolling through posts. Random facts. Cooking videos. Then, I froze.

A post in the form of a video of Ivy popped up on my timeline.

I sat up immediately, turning on the sound without hesitation.

"Let's zero in on the remarkable performance of Marcelo Jordan from last night's clash between the Miami Heat and the Chicago Bulls," her voice said through my device's speakers.

It was a clip from her YouTube channel, which had been growing like wildfire. With so much time spent at home taking care of Baby Love, Ivy had found a way to make boss moves from the home office in Greene Gardens.

"Marcelo wrapped up the game with an impressive 30 points, 10 assists, and five rebounds. But it's not just the stats that tell the story —it's this clutch play in the final quarter that really turned heads."

Unlike her polished, professional look from her on-court days with *Free-Throw Nation*, Ivy recorded her videos stripped-down. Hair in a bun or loose, her face makeup-free, and her outfits simple— usually a tee and leggings. Even without all the glam, she was stunning.

Watching her eyes light up as she spoke about one of her favorite topics, I couldn't stop myself from smiling. My attention kept drifting to her lips—their natural pink hue—and every time she smiled at the camera, my heart did something I didn't quite know how to handle.

The clip ended with her logo and a link to the full video, but I replayed it. Then I replayed it again. And again.

It was funny. Ivy was usually so particular, so detail oriented, a serial perfectionist. But when it came to sports? She was relaxed. Easygoing. Fun. Personable. You just wanted to grab a drink and pick her brain about any team in the NBA.

She was great at what she did because she loved it.

The video was cleanly edited, interspersed with clips of players on the court and highlight reels, thanks to her former cameraman, Jim, who was still helping her out on the side.

I hearted her post and tapped into the comments. Most people praised her for her sports knowledge, but there were a couple that made me pause.

"Not only does Ivy know her stuff better than most commentators out there, but she's also stunning. 😊 A natural beauty. Can't believe someone so beautiful can also break down a game like that! #BeautyAndBrains"

I twisted my lips to one side.

Then I scrolled to another one, and this one? It made my blood pressure rise.

"Damn, baby, I ain't hear a thing you said 😵. You are just too fine!"

I bit back a reaction, but it wasn't easy.

The comments praising Marcelo Jordan or Ivy's insight didn't faze me. But the ones from sleazy guys? Yeah, those got under my skin.

I rolled my tongue around my mouth, feeling a surge of something I didn't want to name—annoyance, jealousy?

"Nah," I muttered aloud.

Because I'd never felt anything like this for any woman in my natural Black life.

But what *was* that feeling? Why did those comments about Ivy bother me so much?

I clicked into Ivy's profile a second later, scanning her social media feed. Her wall was filled with pictures: her at work, her random selfies looking fine as hell whether she was all dolled up or barefaced, and more recently, pictures of her with Baby Love.

I hearted a photo of her sitting at her desk working. Then another, and another.

When I reached the pictures of Ivy capturing Baby Love's milestones, something twisted in my chest. There was one of him lifting his head for the first time, and the one I vividly remembered—the day he rolled over.

"Did you see that?!" she'd shouted, hopping off the couch.

We were all chilling in the living room during one of the rare times I was home.

"He just rolled over," she said, her face lighting up as she turned to me. She jumped up and down, clapping like she'd won the lottery. "Good job, Baby Love! You did it!"

At first, I didn't see what the big deal was. But she explained that Baby Love rolling over at three months was way ahead of schedule. Seeing her light up over something like that, though? It was so damn cute.

I put my phone down on the bed. I had to because sitting here alone in my loft, looking at pictures of Ivy and the baby, brought on a wave of emotions I wasn't prepared for.

Greene Gardens never felt like home. But Ivy and the baby? They kind of did.

The house itself was isolated, far from the city, with barely any infrastructure in the village. I used to feel like I had to leave to find life outside of it. But in that house? The vibe was different. Even though it was hard at times and often made me want to escape, being there had started to mean something.

And now, all I could think about was Ivy.

Seeing her in that video, talking sports with her usual passion, made me miss our late-night conversations. The ones in the kitchen, when her eyes burned with exhaustion but she'd still find something funny to say. It reminded me that life didn't feel so bad when I wasn't doing it alone.

The mornings in Greene Gardens were chaotic. The evenings were a whirlwind with Ivy determined to stick to Baby Love's schedule. And when the house finally quieted down at night, I thought I hated the silence.

But now? I missed it.

"What the fuck is happening?" I mumbled to myself, lying on my back and staring at the ceiling.

And the bigger question: *Could I fix something I might've broken if I didn't want it to stay broken?*

Because here I was, back in my loft—a place I once considered my sanctuary—wanting to go back to the house I thought was a prison. Wanting to be near a woman I had no business wanting.

Ivy and I were co-parents. Sleeping together couldn't lead anywhere good. I didn't do relationships, and Ivy? She did. And if she wanted what other women had wanted from me—commitment—I'd ruin her. She'd hate me.

And we couldn't afford that. Not with what we had to do for Baby Love.

"Shit," I muttered, pressing my fingers to my eyes. "Why the hell can't I sleep?"

Because Ivy, and the life we were building in Greene Gardens, was heavy on my mind.

And I really, really wished it wasn't.

ivy

"GOD, grant me the serenity to accept the things I cannot change, courage to change the things I can..."

I sat in my chair, my eyes scanning the room from left to right, watching mouths move in unison and voices echo around me as a group of strangers recited the Serenity Prayer they clearly said together often.

"...and the wisdom to know the difference..."

Leaning back into the chair, I listened, feeling distinctly out of my element.

I was here—in the basement of a Brooklyn bookstore—because a former colleague swore it could help me.

During one of my emotional breakdowns that were occurring more frequently these days, I had shared with her how overwhelmed I was. Ideas about the future consumed me, and I had no one to confide in since Kendra passed.

"Have you ever heard of Rylee Daniels?" Jayme, my colleague, asked when we met for coffee. I needed to get out of Greene Gardens for a day, so I left Baby Love with the nanny.

"She was Lennox Walker's best friend," she continued.

My brows shot up. "The Bronx Baller who passed away?"

"Mm-hmm." Jayme sipped her coffee. "They had two children together. One before he passed and another shortly after."

"Wait." I sat up straighter. "So they were together?"

"No." She giggled. "Their story is... unique."

"Hmph." I cradled my paper cup of coffee. If their friendship-turned-parenting arrangement was unique, it sounded far too familiar.

"Anyway," Jayme said, "Rylee started a support group in Brooklyn for people who've lost spouses or partners. It's grief counseling or something."

I tilted my head.

"Even though Kendra wasn't your spouse or partner," she added with a small smile, "I think the group could help."

I hadn't believed it would, but after my first meeting, I felt slightly differently.

The room was full of people grieving lost loved ones—partners, spouses, soulmates. While Kendra and I were as close as sisters, I didn't think my situation aligned with anyone else's here... except Rylee's.

After Jayme told me about her and Lennox, I'd looked Rylee up. Jayme was right—their story was unique. It also hit close to home. So, I came to the group. Even if I didn't quite fit the target audience, I needed help, and as my mother reminded me, I had to keep reaching out.

"What do you think about this blouse?" my mother asked, holding up a lime-green silk shirt. "I have so many things I can pair this with."

I'd spent the day with her after calling a car service to visit the city. I'd brought Baby Love along and met up with Leo first to drop him off at Leo's loft for the night.

It was the first time Baby Love would be staying alone with Leo, and I was on edge about it.

Though Leo had improved with all the baby care stuff that had initially intimidated us both, I couldn't shake my nerves. But my mother had convinced me to stop being a helicopter guardian. "Leo's his guardian, too," she said, with her usual directness.

Still, it was hard to focus while shopping with her.

"*Ivy?*" *she called.*

"*Huh?*" *I turned to face her.*

"*The shirt.*" *She held up the blouse again.* "*What do you think?*"

"*It's bright and loud,*" *I replied.* "*It's too much.*"

She smirked. "*So, you hate it?*"

"*Very much,*" *I said.*

"*Perfect.*" *Her smirk turned into a broad smile.* "*I'm getting it, then.*"

I snorted a laugh.

My mother and I were night and day. Her interests couldn't have been further from mine. I swore her free-spirited nature was the reason I craved order and clung to it, trying to avoid being too much like her.

And yet, since becoming Baby Love's guardian, I'd been feeling what I imagined she'd felt as a single mother.

Growing up, it was just my mother and me. My father was never really in the picture; he and my mom never married, ending their relationship soon after I was born. Over the years, he faded into a distant memory I hardly recalled. I can't say I knew him, not really. After all, there's not much to know about someone who's more a shadow than a substance in your life. We've had no contact for years, and while sometimes I wonder about the 'what ifs,' I've come to terms with the quiet space he occupies in my past. My mother filled our lives with enough love and strength for two parents, shaping me into who I am without his influence. Plus, my maternal grandfather when he was alive was the perfect substitute.

"*Why are you so distracted, anyway?*" *she asked, moving through racks of clothes.*

We were in her favorite discount department store. She loved scouring clearance racks, searching for deals that looked far more expensive than their price tags.

I hated these places. Something about the clutter of stuff jammed together on racks gave me low-level anxiety.

"*I'm not distracted, Mommy. I'm scared.*"

She stopped sliding hangers on the clothing rod to give me her full attention.

"Is this about you leaving the baby with Leo today?" my mother asked, her tone soft but probing. "Because I'm sure he's more than capable, Ivy."

"It's not just that." I sighed, leaning against one of the clothing racks for support. "I'm scared for the baby's future. He doesn't even have a name. He's almost four months old. If Leo and I can't work together to come up with something as simple as a name for this child, how are we supposed to work together to raise him into a well-rounded adult?"

My mother stared at me for a moment before bursting into laughter.

I straightened, crossing my arms tightly over my chest. "Oh, I'm so glad my existential crisis is funny to you."

She held up a hand, still giggling as she tried to catch her breath. "I'm sorry, baby. I really am."

"Mm-hmm." My tone was flat, though the corner of my mouth twitched. "And I really am happy to be your personal comedy hour."

"It's just..." She took another deep breath, finally composing herself. "This is so you. You'd let something like this weigh you down when you're already doing so much right." She reached out, brushing my cheek with her warm hand. "Ivy, listen to me. You have an excellent support system. You've got the baby's grandparents, Leo's mother, and me. You are not doing this alone."

I sighed, the weight of her words making me feel both comforted and uneasy.

"You are never really alone, as long as you keep reaching out," she continued, her thumb brushing my cheek before her hand dropped away. She turned back to the clothing rack, sliding hangers along the metal bar with determination. "You've got to get in the habit of asking for help. Stop expecting to do everything by yourself. It really does take a village."

We fell into a brief silence, and I tried to let her words sink in. But instead, the truth burst out before I could stop myself. "Leo and I slept together."

She froze mid-reach, slowly turning her head to stare at me.

"Twice," I added, my voice barely above a whisper. "It was probably why he moved back to his loft."

My mother blinked, her eyes wide. "Oh."

"And now he's been liking all my pictures on social media," I said, frustration creeping into my voice, "but barely says two words to me when we're face-to-face. Like earlier, when I handed the baby off to him."

Her jaw dropped slightly, and she looked around, as if needing to confirm she'd heard me right. "Oh."

"It was a mistake," I admitted, shaking my head. "I've resolved to forgive myself for it. We aren't in a good place since he moved out, but honestly, it's probably for the best."

"Hmph." She tilted her head, giving me that knowing look she's perfected over the years. "Well, I like him."

I rolled my eyes, exasperated. "Mommy, please."

"He's handsome and very successful," she said, as if I hadn't spoken. "And single. And handsome. Did I mention he's handsome?"

"It's not happening again," I said firmly, shaking my head. "So don't even start."

She smiled, turning back to the rack with a shrug. "Okay... if you say so."

"I do say so," I insisted.

"Mm-hmm."

"Anyway," I said, trying to steer the conversation away, "what happened between us is what's got me feeling so unsure. How can I handle being a single parent—or guardian—or whatever—if I'm already this thrown off?"

"You've got a village," she reminded me, her tone softening. "It's not going to be easy. But life never is. There are mountains and valleys, Ivy. It's your perspective that makes the difference. How you choose to travel those paths is what separates the happy from the sad." She turned to face me fully. "You are never alone, as long as you keep reaching out."

Encouraged by her words, I found the strength to approach Rylee after the group session.

She was a joy to watch, gracefully engaging with everyone who came up to her. I'd heard from others that there was usually a therapist leading the group, but today, Rylee seemed to take on that role effortlessly. Her presence was warm and inviting.

As she gathered a stack of loose papers from the table, I cleared my throat. "Hey—hi, Rylee."

She looked up, and a smile spread across her face. "Hey, Ivy."

I gasped softly, surprised she knew my name. "Oh! How... how do you—"

She turned the papers in her hand to show me. "You signed in when you got here. I know everyone else's name on this list since they're regulars. Yours was the only new one. And since you didn't say much during the meeting, I figured you had to be Ivy."

I laughed, impressed. "Very observant."

"Oh, girl." She giggled, tucking the papers under her arm. "I try. So, how was your first meeting with us today?"

"It was good." I nodded, meaning it. "You've created an environment that feels really safe."

That last word came out as a tremble as a sudden wave of emotions hit me.

Rylee immediately noticed, placing the stack of papers back on the table. "Oh, Ivy, are you okay?"

I nodded quickly, inhaling deeply to keep the tears at bay. "I'm just... I'm really grateful for this space right now. Especially right now."

Rylee gave me her full attention, her expression calm and inviting. She didn't rush me to explain or try to fill the silence. She simply let me speak.

"I... I didn't lose a spouse," I admitted softly. "I lost my best friend. A woman who I considered to be my sister. So much so, I agreed to be her baby's godmother when she asked me—two weeks after learning she was pregnant."

Rylee nodded gently, encouraging me to continue.

"But then," I said, my voice faltering as I pressed a hand to my neck, "weeks before she was due to give birth..." I took a shaky breath, feeling the tears slipping free, "she and her husband died in a car accident."

"Oh, God." Rylee's tone softened as she reached into her bag, retrieving a sheet of tissue. "Here," she said, holding it out to me.

I took it gratefully, pressing it to my eyes. "She had a will," I continued. "In it, she named me and our friend—her husband's best friend—as guardians of a baby neither of us knew anything about raising."

"Wow," Rylee said, the weight of her breath matching the weight in her tone.

"And I just feel like I've been drowning in everything since I got the news."

Rylee placed a hand gently on my shoulder. "Let's sit," she said, guiding me to a pair of chairs near the now-empty meeting area.

Through the pill-sized windows of the basement, I could see shoes tapping along the sidewalk above us, the sound faint but steady. The world above carried on, but for a moment, it felt like just the two of us here.

"I can't help feeling like I have no idea what I'm doing," I confessed, dabbing at my eyes. "It feels like I'm making it all up as I go. I've read every baby book, every parenting guide. And while they make me feel like I could conquer a classroom of toddlers..."

Rylee chuckled softly.

"...they don't talk about the exhaustion, the doubt, or the imposter syndrome," I continued. "Which I'm already familiar with, being a sports commentator for a living."

Rylee's eyes lit up. "Wait—*Free-Throw Nation*? That's you, isn't it? I knew you looked familiar, but I couldn't place it!"

"Yeah." I sighed, running a hand through my hair. "But you probably didn't recognize me because I look a mess these days. And, honestly, I haven't cared too much about that lately."

"You look amazing," she said sincerely, nodding for emphasis. "And trust me, I know exactly what you're going through. It gets better."

She turned more toward me, her posture softening. "I was exactly where you are now. Grieving the loss of my best friend—the one person I'd known since before I could walk or talk. We had just had a baby months before his passing. My oldest was barely one when he died." She paused, her voice trembling slightly. "And if that wasn't enough, I found out I was pregnant again not long after his funeral."

"Wow." I shook my head, swallowing hard.

"It was a lot. Almost too much. But you know what saved me?" She leaned forward slightly. "Community. There was an outpouring of help, more than I even knew what to do with. And for once in my life, I didn't refuse it. I had to learn that while no one could take away the pain I was feeling, they could help with the everyday things so I'd have the space to process it all."

I nodded, her words hitting close to home.

"I wanted to curl up, shut everyone out, and deal with it all on my own. But I had to let people in. Because even though no one could truly understand what I was going through, they still wanted to help. And that made all the difference."

I scoffed softly. "My mother said the same thing."

Rylee smiled knowingly. "Sounds like your mom is a wise woman."

"She has her moments," I admitted.

Rylee giggled.

"The good news," Rylee continued, "is that it does get better. The bad news is that the pain? It never really goes away."

I pressed my lips together, letting her words sink in.

"The grief pops up at the most random times," she explained. "Not just on anniversaries or birthdays, but in the smallest, most unexpected moments. And that's okay. My therapist taught me to feel it—to acknowledge it—and then to send it off with love. How you do that is up to you. For me, it's hugging my babies, showering them with kisses until they're sick of me."

I laughed quietly, the image warming my heart.

"For others, it's visiting their loved one's favorite spot or simply letting themselves cry. And that's okay too. Crying is a release, and sometimes it's all you can do."

I nodded, my throat tightening with emotion.

"Losing a best friend is hard," she said, her voice soft but steady. "But they never really leave you. And as long as you remember that, you're never truly alone. Not physically. Not spiritually. You're one step closer to finding the peace you need."

I dabbed at the last of my tears, her words resonating deeply. "Thank you, Rylee. Your words... they've helped more than you know."

Rylee smiled warmly. "Good. I always wished there was a space where I could hear something that made the world feel like it made sense again. I'm glad to be that for you."

She stood and walked to the table she'd been organizing earlier. "Hey, I'd love it if we exchanged numbers. That way, we can stay in touch."

"Yeah, absolutely." I stood quickly, following her to the table.

We exchanged numbers, and just like that, the weight I'd been carrying felt a little lighter.

* * *

I stood in the middle of the living room, a strange realization settling over me—I had nothing to do.

I'd just finished recording a commentary video for my channel, something I'd planned to edit later, but right now, I didn't feel like it. Baby Love had been down for his nap for almost an hour, and I'd planned to use the free time to clean the house after recording.

Except... there was nothing to clean.

I looked around the living room, blinking at the spotless space. It was quiet—almost too quiet.

There were no sneakers scattered by the entryway, no sweaty T-shirts draped over the couch. The socks that used to spill out of shoes weren't there either. Everything was perfectly in place. And to my surprise, I didn't like it.

I let out a small, disbelieving laugh as I dropped onto the couch, tilting my head back to rest against the back cushions.

Was I... missing Leo? Missing his messy ass?

The thought made me laugh again, but it didn't feel ridiculous. No matter how annoyed I'd been by his clutter, his presence gave the house life. It felt lived in when he was here. Now, it felt like a showroom—a perfect display, polished and untouched.

When Leo told me he was moving back to his loft, my heart sank. And when he actually left, it sank even further.

It wasn't just about him being gone. Him moving out meant Baby Love would stay with him sometimes at the loft. That idea didn't sit well with me. Greene Gardens was baby-proofed, carefully organized for a child's safety. His loft? It was a bachelor pad. As far as baby-proofing went, it barely had a working lock on the door.

But we'd both agreed that things between us had become too tense. For the sake of co-parenting, space was supposed to be the solution. We hadn't formalized anything legally, just a verbal agreement for now.

His absence gave me the time to do things I hadn't been able to do since taking on the guardianship—like visiting my mom or attending a grief support group. It was freeing in a way. Yet now, in the quiet of the house, I found myself... restless.

I turned my head, my gaze falling on the hallway that led to the home office. The idea of editing the video I'd just recorded crossed my mind, but my motivation was already gone.

Instead, another thought surfaced. I'd been telling myself for weeks that I needed to clear out the walk-in closet in the master bedroom. My clothes were still in a makeshift setup, crammed into drawers or stored in the office. It was inconvenient, especially with an event coming up in a few days. But for the event, I wanted to have everything waiting for me in one place as I got ready. The last thing I wanted was to interrupt my routine by trekking up and down the stairs to grab an outfit.

With a sigh, I pushed myself off the couch and headed upstairs to the bedroom, determined to make use of my free time.

When I opened the closet doors, the sight made me freeze.

Boxes.

Kendra and Tyrell's belongings were piled high—big boxes stacked on top of each other, smaller ones nestled wherever they fit.

I blew air through my lips, the vibration a sound of defeat.

"Where the hell do I start?"

The labels on the boxes were clear: Kendra's clothes, shoes, and accessories. There were so many of them, and I could already hear her voice joking about her shopping habits. She was so much like my mother in that way.

"I need to start small," I muttered to myself with a small laugh, shaking my head as I rolled up my sleeves.

Because if I tackled the bigger boxes first, I'd get overwhelmed before I made any progress.

My eyes scanned the labels as I leaned forward, hunching down here and there to read them. Among the piles, one box stood out: *Baby Stuff.*

"Hmph," I muttered to myself. "I thought we told them to put anything labeled 'baby' in the nursery."

Leo and I had given the movers clear instructions when they brought everything to Greene Gardens. Kendra and Tyrell had already packed most of their belongings, planning to move in after their baby shower and right before Baby Love was born. The apartment they left behind required minimal handling—Leo and I closed out the lease and ensured everything was tied up.

At the Greene Gardens house, we told the movers to pile everything in the walk-in closet except for the boxes marked "baby," which were supposed to go straight into the nursery. But somehow, this one hadn't made it.

"I guess I'm starting with you," I said softly, my eyes fixed on the label.

It felt like the logical place to begin. Anything for the baby could be useful now or in the near future.

I sank onto the closet floor, the plush carpet cushioning my knees as I began pulling at the box's taped tabs. It was tightly sealed, but I managed to pry it open after a little struggle.

Inside, I found packaged onesies, a blank photo album, baby books, and a long strip of ultrasound photos.

The sight of the ultrasound photos stopped me cold.

I remembered them vividly—Kendra's way of announcing her pregnancy to Leo and me. My eyes had bugged out when she presented the pictures, her joy infectious. I'd been excited for her, but I'd also felt a pang of fear.

I worried the baby would change things between us, pulling her away from our friendship. So many women I knew had drifted away after becoming mothers, consumed by the demands of their new lives. I feared I'd lose her to late-night feedings and playdates.

I exhaled, shaking off the memory, and continued unpacking.

As I worked through the items in the box, my hand landed on a Moleskine notebook. I grabbed it by the cover, intending to set it aside, but something stopped me.

Words.

Written in Kendra's handwriting were paragraphs of sentences that spilled out when the book fell open on the carpeted floor.

Curiosity drew my eyes to the page.

I can't believe in just a few months we'll meet our little miracle. This journey has been nothing short of magic, filled with dreams of little footsteps that will soon echo through our home.

The sentence hit me like a wave, halting my movements.

She kept a journal?

I didn't even know she liked journaling.

I lifted the notebook, holding it in my lap. As I flipped through the pages, I realized this wasn't just a random journal. It was intentional. A diary documenting her pregnancy. These pages held Kendra's deepest thoughts—things she'd never shared with me.

Her fears about labor. The quiet anxiety every time she went to the bathroom, praying she wouldn't see blood. Her excitement and joy about becoming a mother.

I skimmed over her entries, smiling at her words, stopping to read sections that tugged at me more.

Then I turned to a page near the end of the journal.

If we have a girl, Tyrell and I decided we'd name her Violet. It's pretty and classy like Ivy, and contains four important letters. Vi and Le. Letters in Ivy and Leo. It's a little piece of our friends' names, whose support has meant the world to me.

"Oh my God," I whispered, my jaw dropping.

My eyes moved down the page to the next section.

If it's a boy, Levi it is. It's strong but soft, just like Leo. It also has both the first letters of their godparents' names. I hope he grows up with Leo's strength and Ivy's grace.

I pressed the journal against my chest, shutting my eyes tightly as tears escaped, sliding down my cheeks.

"Levi," I whispered, tasting the name. "I love it."

I had thought I'd never know what Kendra and Tyrell wanted to name their baby. They'd kept it a secret, wanting it to be a surprise.

Finding the journal—and their chosen names—felt like a gift I hadn't expected.

A wave of gratitude swept over me. Leo and I had held off on naming Baby Love, and now I was so thankful we had.

I pulled the journal away from my chest, my tear-filled eyes returning to the page. I read further, soaking in her words.

I still believe Ivy and Leo are meant to be, more than they know. Being godparents and sometimes needing to work together when Tyrell and I ask them to might just show them the beautiful bond they share but that they've yet to uncover.

I crumpled into a mess of sobs.

For months, I'd wished I could pick up the phone and call her, desperate to hear her voice again. She wasn't just my best friend— she was my sister. My only true confidant.

If she were here, she would've been the first person I called after both hookups with Leo.

And I just knew if she were still here, she would holler with laughter and pepper me with "I told you so."

Reading her journal reminded me of how deeply my friend understood things—often beyond what I could comprehend. Her insistence that Leo and I were perfect for each other had always seemed ridiculous to me. We were polar opposites in so many ways. But now... I wasn't so sure.

Because the truth was, I did have feelings for him. Feelings that had only grown stronger since we'd been intimate.

As much as I wanted to pretend that him moving out made it easier to maintain a clean, quiet, organized environment... the reality was, I missed him.

A lot.

It wasn't just his presence I missed. I missed his touch.

We'd only done it twice, but already I could feel the ache of withdrawal.

We'd kept things cordial enough when I'd dropped the baby off at his loft so I could hang out with my mom and attend the grief support meeting. But even in those brief interactions, it was hard to ignore the truth I couldn't avoid admitting now: I missed him.

Sniffling, I wiped my tears, preparing to keep reading the last few journal entries from Kendra when I heard the baby wake from his nap.

The sound of his little voice, babbling and cooing, pulled my attention instantly.

A smile spread across my lips as I pushed myself up from the carpet, making my way to his nursery.

"Hey… Levi," I said the moment I stepped into the room, his little eyes found mine, and his face lit up with a big, gummy smile.

"Oh, you like that, huh?" I whispered softly, my chest tightening with the kind of love I never thought I'd feel for anyone, let alone a baby.

I leaned over the crib railing, placing my hand gently on his soft, round belly. "Levi."

His smile widened at the sound of the name, and my heart swelled.

"You like that, don't you?" I asked, my voice catching with emotion. "Good. Because you look like a Levi."

I scooped him up, planting a kiss on his chubby little cheek. He responded by brushing his hand against my face, his tiny fingers grazing my skin.

My heart melted.

If someone had told me a year ago that I would fall head over heels in love with a baby, I would have laughed in their face. I thought I didn't like kids. I'd never been around them before Levi.

But Levi had changed everything.

"Let's get you your bottle," I said softly, cradling him as I headed to the bottle warmer.

Once it was ready, I sat down with him in the rocking chair, settling him in a comfortable position as I offered him his milk.

The room was quiet except for the soft sounds of Levi drinking, the rhythmic creak of the rocking chair, and the warmth of his tiny body resting against mine.

As I held him, my thoughts drifted back to the final words, Kendra's last journal entry, that I'd read in Kendra's journal before I had to leave it behind to tend to Levi.

I've always believed names carry power and influence. Tyrell and I decided to choose names that had the same letters as our friends' names to prove how good they look together. Giving you this name serves two purposes, little one. It's to show you that you are loved beyond your mom and dad, and it's to serve as a hope that one day, Ivy and Leo will see the love between them that Daddy and Mommy saw in them—that we still believe to this day was meant to be.

Tears stung my eyes again, but this time, they were accompanied by a small, hopeful smile.

Kendra had made a promise to be that person for Levi, to ensure he always knew he was loved. And now, I was determined to keep that promise for her.

Which meant I needed to mend things with Leo, too.

Because maybe—just maybe—we could be the family Kendra envisioned she and Tyrell being to Levi.

Maybe.

SEVENTEEN

APPLAUSE RANG out around the large room as my name was called at the podium.

I was at the Annual NBA Honors, an event that recognized the league's top performers for the regular season. Tonight, I was being awarded *Most Improved Player*, a recognition that made every single late night and grueling practice feel worth it.

Smiling at the people around me, I exchanged daps with a few teammates and others nearby before standing and making my way to the stage. Pride swelled in my chest with every step, because I knew I'd earned this.

When I reached the stage, I shook the commissioner's hand and accepted the award with the other. We turned and posed for the waiting photographers, snapping photos at lightening speed.

The award was heavier than I expected, its sleek design catching the lights from the room. My name was etched in gold on the black marbled base, and a silver basketball seemed to burst through a clear crystal plane—like breaking through barriers. It felt like a symbol of the journey I'd taken this season.

The smile on my face only grew as I stared at it for a moment.

When I signed with the Bronx Ballers eight years ago as a rookie,

I knew I wanted to be more than just another player on the roster. I wanted to matter to the team. And I'd worked my ass off to make that happen, even through personal losses and challenges I wouldn't wish on anyone.

Placing the trophy on the podium, I turned to face the crowd. The applause slowly quieted, and I leaned toward the mic.

"Thank you," I began, my voice steady but full of emotion. "I wrote a speech because if you know me, you know I don't do well with public speaking... unless I'm yelling across the court."

The room erupted in laughter, and I chuckled along with them, the sound easing some of the tension in my chest.

I wasn't nervous exactly—I'd spoken in front of crowds plenty of times—but excitement had a way of tangling my words if I wasn't careful.

The night was perfect. A cool spring evening. The large hall in Manhattan was packed with some of the best in the NBA, all gathered to celebrate the hard work and talent that defined the season.

The Bronx Ballers hadn't made the playoffs this year, and yeah, that stung. I'd thought this would be our year. But looking back, I knew we'd given it our all. Injuries, bad games, and my own mental struggles after losing Tyrell and Kendra had tested me in ways I wasn't sure I'd pass.

And yet, I'd shown up.

"Ladies and gentlemen," I said, glancing down at the paper in my hand. "First and foremost, I'd like to extend my heartfelt thanks to the NBA and the sports journalists for this incredible honor. Receiving the Most Improved Player Award is a testament not just to my efforts, but to the unwavering support and hard work of my teammates, coaches, and the entire staff of the Bronx Ballers."

I glanced up briefly, saluting a few of my teammates in the crowd. My gaze swept the room, searching for familiar faces—and then I saw her.

Ivy.

She was seated at one of the tables in the back, her smile radiant even from across the room.

I froze for a second, my heart stumbling over itself as her presence washed over me.

She was here.

I bit down on my bottom lip, swallowing the unexpected lump in my throat, and forced my eyes back to the paper.

"This season has been a journey of growth, challenges, and relentless pursuit of excellence," I continued. "Despite our team not making the playoffs, we've all pushed each other to be better every day. This award, while it might bear my name, really belongs to the entire organization for believing in me, pushing me, and supporting my growth both on and off the court."

The applause came again, and I nodded my thanks, feeling a wave of gratitude for the people who had my back this season.

When the room settled, I glanced up again, my eyes drifting back to Ivy's table as I continued.

"I also want to thank my family and friends for their unconditional love and support," I said, locking eyes with her this time. "Your faith in me fuels my drive to improve and to represent our values every time I step on the court."

She smiled softly, and the warmth of that simple gesture filled me with more pride than the award in my hands.

I hadn't expected anyone to be here for me tonight. It wasn't the kind of event I usually invited my mom or extended family to. Often Tyrell would be the only person I'd tell about it, and he'd always show up. And Ivy... Ivy never came to ceremonies like this, even when she was invited.

But here she was.

"Lastly," I said, gripping the trophy and lifting it slightly, "I want to dedicate this award to my late friends, Kendra and Tyrell, whose memories inspire me to make the most of every moment. They taught me that improvement isn't just about skills on the court but about growing as a person and making a positive impact in the lives of others. Thank you for this honor, and I promise to continue working hard to live up to it."

The room erupted into applause, and I stepped back from the mic, glancing once more at Ivy before leaving the stage.

Applause rang out louder around the room, the sound rising to a standing ovation. Surrounded by players, coaches, and others in the crowd, I tried to spot Ivy again, craning my neck to see through the gaps of people standing around me. She was one of the tiniest women I knew, and as the sea of faces moved, she seemed to disappear in the mix.

I hope I can speak with her.

Since I'd moved out of Greene Gardens, things between Ivy and me had smoothed over—at least on the surface. Communication had been better, particularly when it came to handing off Baby Love. Whenever I had him for the weekend or after practices during the last stretch of the season, we coordinated easily. Now, with the season over and playoffs beginning, I was looking forward to more time with the baby.

As soon as I stepped down from the podium, I was met with congratulations and firm pats on the back. After leaving my award at my table, I wove through the crowd toward the back of the room, scanning for Ivy. I hadn't seen her since the week before, when I returned Baby Love to Greene Gardens after he spent his third night with me. Co-parenting had been manageable this way, but there were nights I missed being able to wake up, wander down the hall, and sit in the rocking chair near his crib, just watching him sleep.

I'd put together a small nursery in my loft, complete with a crib and changing table beside my bed, but it didn't feel the same.

When I found Ivy, she was mid-conversation with a colleague, a glass of champagne in her hand and a radiant smile on her red painted lips. She looked effortlessly elegant in an all-black, one-shoulder pantsuit. The cape-like sleeve added a touch of drama, draping past her thighs and cinching her waist in a way that made me want to stop and stare. Classy, stylish, and every bit Ivy Pressman.

"Hey," I said, my voice directed to her hips before I raised my eyes to meet hers.

She turned, a polite smile tugging at her lips as she excused herself from her colleague. He nodded at me and wished me congratulations as he stepped away.

"Hey, you," Ivy greeted me, using her clutch to lightly tap my arm. "Congratulations."

"Thank you." I grinned. "You almost knocked me off my game up there during my speech."

"What?" She pressed her hand to her chest, feigning surprise. "How?"

"I wasn't expecting you to be here."

Her smile returned, soft yet bright. "Come on, Leo. I wasn't going to miss it. It's not your first award, but this one was earned. A clear testament to how hard you worked this season." She winked. "Plus, I voted for you. I wanted to see my vote give his speech."

I chuckled, tossing my head back. "Aight, makes sense."

"And," she continued, her expression softening as her eyes clouded slightly, "I just know Tyrell would've been here with bells on."

I nodded, swallowing hard as I sniffed back the sting of emotion creeping into my nose. Seeing Ivy in the crowd tonight had meant more than just her professional presence. Things between us hadn't been the same since... since the last time we had sex. I hadn't stopped thinking about her or what had happened between us, but I wasn't sure if she had. That uncertainty lingered, making her presence here unexpected and oddly comforting.

"So," I started, forcing my voice steady, "who's watching the baby?"

"Tyrell's mom," she said with a nod. "She said her hip was feeling much better, so she insisted on driving out to Greene Gardens to spend time with him when I mentioned the awards ceremony. So, she's there now watching the baby... who we can now call Levi."

I furrowed my brows, confused. "Levi?"

Ivy drew in a deep breath and placed her hand on her chest. "I found this box that the movers didn't put in the nursery. It was labeled 'Baby Stuff' and somehow ended up in the master bedroom closet. I got bored one night and decided to start sorting through it."

"Okay..." I encouraged, my interest piqued.

"Kendra kept a journal in that box," Ivy explained, her voice warm with reminiscence. "I read a few pages—bawling my eyes out, of course. There was so much she never shared with me..." She shook her head, waving her free hand as if to dismiss the overwhelming emotions. "Anyway, in that journal, she wrote about the names she and Tyrell had chosen if the baby were a boy or a girl. And if it was a boy, they decided to name him Levi."

I blinked, my jaw slack as the weight of her words sank in. "That's... amazing."

"Right?!" Ivy's lips trembled as she forced in a breath, holding her composure. "She wrote about why they chose Levi. She said they wanted us to feel close to him. That they chose the name because it combined parts of *our* names—your 'L' and 'E,' and my 'V' and 'I.'" Her voice wavered. "She wanted him to carry a piece of us, to remind us how much they loved us."

The room seemed to fade around us, the distant hum of voices and laughter falling into the background.

Ivy's eyes glistened as she continued. "She wanted to wait to reveal the baby's name after he was born so she could explain why they chose it. She hoped it would help us embrace the change he'd bring into our lives by helping us to see parts of us in him by way of his name."

I nodded slowly, unable to form words in the moment. The revelation settled heavily on my chest, equal parts bittersweet and awe-inspiring.

I couldn't believe what I was hearing. I hadn't been as hung up on choosing a name for the baby the way Ivy had been, but it really meant something that we were going to give him the name his parents wanted.

"I haven't reached out to the estate lawyer with the news or made any filings," she informed. "I wanted to tell you first and make sure we both agree on the name before we start adding it to the birth certificate, birth records, and all that jazz."

"Ivy, Leo," a voice called from the side of us. When I turned my head, I saw a photographer we knew, Talia, with a massive camera lens aimed in our direction. "Can I get a photo of the most famous friends in the room?"

Ivy laughed softly. "Famous friends? Talia, you do too much."

Talia grinned at her, then turned to me.

"Sure, T," I said, taking a step closer to Ivy. "And you dubbed us accurately. Just make sure you get my good side."

"All sides of you are good, LV," Talia teased, raising the camera to her face.

I looped an arm around Ivy's waist and pulled her close, closing the distance between us for the photo. I underestimated the effect of feeling her body against mine—she fit so perfectly, like she was supposed to be here. The camera flashes flickered, and I smiled, keeping my gaze forward.

Talia stepped back, lowering the camera to inspect the photos she'd taken. A satisfied grin spread across her face. "Y'all look amazing. Thank you!"

Ivy stepped out of my hold, clearing her throat, and looked up at me with a small smile.

I shifted slightly, trying to keep my body calm. To say I hadn't been thinking of Ivy in that way—about the nights we spent together—would've been a straight-up lie. Every night since then, memories of her had come rushing back. The way she looked at me, the way her body moved with mine, taking in every inch I gave, the sounds she made… it all kept playing on a loop in my head. At first, I tried to fight those thoughts. Now, I didn't even bother.

"So, this weekend, right?" she asked, snapping me out of my thoughts. "Levi"—her lips curved into a small grin as she said his name—"will be with you?"

I nodded. "Yup."

"Cool." She nodded again, shifting the clutch under her arm and gesturing toward the exit. "I'm gonna—"

"Do you... wanna grab a drink... or something?"

The words spilled out before I could stop them.

She tilted her head, studying me. "Or something?"

I licked my lips and shrugged. "Yeah."

"What's the *something*?"

I chuckled nervously, running a hand down my mouth.

She gasped, then let out a laugh, her smile softening the tension between us. "Ah, so *that's* how you do it. The Leo Vanguard way of getting ladies to make questionable decisions."

Her gaze met mine, her dark eyes locking me in place. The rest of the room faded—the crowd, the noise, everything. All I saw was her. All I wanted was her.

"Leo," a familiar voice called from behind me, breaking the moment.

I turned to see Simeon, my agent, walking toward us. His eyes bounced between Ivy and me, his expression curious.

"Oh," Simeon said, placing a hand over his chest. "Am I interrupting—"

"No," Ivy cut in with a polite smile, glancing at me. "I was just leaving."

I held her gaze, not wanting her to go.

She stepped closer to me, balancing on her toes to plant a kiss on my cheek. Instinctively, I wrapped an arm around her waist, pulling her tighter against me. She let out a soft sound that nearly undid me.

"I'll call you," she whispered against my ear.

"Ivy, we need to talk," I said quickly, keeping her close.

With a little more effort, she slipped out of my hold, brushing her thumb along my cheek to clear away the faint red mark her lipstick had left. "I'll call you," she repeated, her voice firm but gentle.

Before I could say anything else, she turned toward Simeon, giving him a quick air kiss and hug before continuing toward the exit.

My eyes stayed on her as she moved through the room, stopping to exchange farewells with colleagues and familiar faces along the way.

"Shit," Simeon said as my attention lingered on Ivy's retreating figure. "Did I interrupt... whatever was happening just now?"

"Nah," I exhaled, forcing my focus back on him. "She was leaving already."

Simeon's eyes scanned my face briefly before I playfully tapped his chest.

"You good?" he asked, tilting his head slightly as if to read me better. "Like, honestly, are you good?"

"I'm great, man. I promise," I lied, gesturing toward the award sitting a few tables away. "Don't I have every reason to be?"

Simeon nodded slowly, though his gaze didn't waver. "Yes, you sure do." He then turned to gesture toward the front of the room. "I've got someone I want you to meet." He gave me a quick pat on the back. "Let's go."

As we started walking, I glanced back one last time, half expecting Ivy to be gone from sight. But just as I did, she turned the corner near the exit and glanced back, catching me looking at her.

She smiled—one of those soft, knowing smiles that hit me square in the chest—and giggled before disappearing around the corner.

That smile stayed with me, and I couldn't ignore the clarity that hit me in that moment. We couldn't just be friends, or co-guardians, or anything as simple as that. There was more between us. There had to be.

* * *

The sound of basketballs bouncing unevenly across the hardwood echoed in the vast space of the training facility.

Though the Bronx Ballers were out of the playoffs, a few of us had gathered at the team's facility to keep up with practice and training during the off-season. This routine had been my focus every year, and it was the reason I'd earned the award I accepted last night.

Still, my mind kept drifting back to that award ceremony, to Ivy.

I thought about calling her when I got back to my loft but decided against it. Things between us had been left on a decent note, and I didn't want to risk ruining the vibe. It had felt so natural talking to her again, just the two of us, like old times before life changed everything.

The indoor court was calm despite the occasional bounce of balls or the swish of a net. I was sharing a hoop with Jaleel Gordon, our shooting guard and one of the most disciplined players on the team.

"Got any plans after this?" I asked as I chased down the ball I'd just shot.

"Rest," Jaleel replied with a grin before launching a clean shot into the hoop. "Promised my wife we'd spend some time together since our kids are with their grandma for the weekend."

"Dope," I said, nodding as I lined up my next shot.

"How about you?"

"I'm heading back to the loft," I said, dribbling the ball lightly. "Gonna clean up a little before driving out to Greene Gardens to pick up the baby." I smiled as I thought about it. "He's spending the weekend with me."

"Love to hear it," Jaleel said with an approving nod.

For a moment, only the rhythmic sound of basketballs bouncing filled the space.

"You think you're gonna move back out there?" Jaleel asked, glancing at me as he lined up another shot.

I sighed, holding the ball against my hip. "I mean, sometimes I miss it, but... Ivy and I have been cool since I moved back to the city. So, I don't know."

"Hmph." Jaleel nodded, his focus shifting back to the hoop.

Most of my teammates knew the basics of the situation with Ivy —how we'd become guardians to Baby Love, now Levi, and how things hadn't worked out living together. What they didn't know was how close we'd gotten. How intimate. That wasn't something I'd shared, not even with Jaleel, though he was one of the few I trusted.

"Yo," I called out. "Can I ask you something personal?"

Jaleel paused mid-dribble and turned to face me, his expression curious. "Depends. How personal we talking?"

I chuckled. "Nothing like that."

"Oh, aight." He let out a relieved laugh. "Go ahead, then."

"How'd you know you wanted to get married and have kids?"

His smile grew softer, his eyes shifting as if he were looking at a memory. "When every time I thought about the future, I saw my girl in it. My wife now," he corrected. "And our kids. Every time."

I arched a brow. "Every time?"

"Every single time, man." Jaleel shot the ball, the perfect arc sending it cleanly through the hoop. He jogged off to retrieve it. "Eva and I got married mad young."

"Yeah, I know," I said, bouncing the ball in place as I waited for him to return.

"And while for some people, it was too young, for me, I just knew what I wanted," he continued. "Now, I won't lie and say it's been perfect. My woman put me out and asked for a divorce at the peak of my career. That shit was devastating."

I stopped dribbling, my attention squarely on him.

"I was living in the city alone, going to events alone, trying to accept that we were separated and that it was what she wanted." He shook his head, holding the ball loosely at his side. "I wasn't in any position to give her what she needed—my time. And I hated every minute of being away from her and J.R. I'd get him on weekends, just like you get the baby, but every time he had to go back, it was like a piece of me went with him. And I wanted to go home too."

He turned to grab the ball that had rolled a few feet away.

"It was our son that brought us back together," Jaleel said, his voice softening as he smiled. "And every time I think about that, I'm proud. Proud of me and Eva for raising a kid who's so damn self-aware, thoughtful, and smart as hell."

I chuckled, shaking my head. "That's dope."

"Since then, I've learned how to make everyone happy," Jaleel said, tossing the ball casually into the air and catching it. "The team, by showing up and giving it my all—even when we lose."

"True."

"My wife, by giving her enough time so she doesn't feel like a single wife anymore," he added with a snicker. "And, of course, my kids. I'm around a lot more now, especially with our baby girl in the picture. She's the cutest little terrorist you've ever seen."

I threw my head back, laughing.

"I make it work for a family that keeps me grounded," he said. "They're my foundation. See, here?" He gestured to the hardwood floor beneath us. "The fans? They only love me when I'm winning. My family? They love me for me, no conditions. That's why they come first. I don't ever wanna get put out my house again, bro."

His laugh was contagious, and I found myself nodding along.

"When I was alone in that quiet-ass condo in Manhattan, every night I wanted to go back home. Feel me?"

"Yeah," I said, my nod slower this time. "I mean, sometimes... I wanna go back to Greene Gardens, too. But..." I trailed off, shaking my head.

"But what?" he asked, turning his full attention to me.

I bit the inside of my cheek, debating for a moment before stepping closer. "I'm gonna tell you something, but you can't repeat it to anyone."

"Say less." Jaleel nodded solemnly. "I'm a vault."

I drew in a deep breath, then let it out. "Me and Ivy... we took our friendship to a whole different level after we moved into Greene Gardens together."

"Oh." Jaleel's eyebrows shot up. "Oh! Y'all never—"

"No."

"Oh," he repeated, nodding slowly. "'Cause... I figured you two already—"

"Never," I said firmly. "Ever, ever. I've never seen her like that before, and to my knowledge, she's never seen me like that either. Our friends used to swear we were perfect for each other, but after our first date, it was clear—we weren't."

"Well..." Jaleel grinned slyly. "Y'all were a match enough to take it to another level."

I sighed, rubbing the inner corners of my eyes. "Things just... shifted when we moved into that house. She started to look different to me, man. And I don't even know how to describe it—"

"Oh, I get it." Jaleel's grin widened. "You were used to vibing with her on the easy stuff, but when you go through hard shit together? That's different. It's only natural things would change. Y'all get each other in a way no one else does. And no one ever will."

"Yeah, but if things change too much, it could risk everything," I countered. "We've got a kid depending on us to get along. Since we took things further, we've argued more. Her feelings are involved—"

"And you haven't been sensitive to them?" Jaleel cut in, folding his arms. "You've been treating her like the other women you deal with?"

I stayed quiet.

"You can't do that, LV." He tapped my chest. "Come on. You know better."

"I've never fucked a friend before," I admitted, laughing nervously.

Jaleel tossed his head back, his laugh echoing across the court.

"I don't even have female friends like that," I added, chuckling. "I'm used to women being interests, not friends. Ivy was different. She ended up in the friend box because we both understood we'd never be anything other than friends. And then we crossed the line. It was great—better than great—but I just know, if I settle into that and try to juggle everything else, I'm gonna fuck it up."

"Have more confidence in yourself."

I shook my head and mumbled, "You sound like my mother."

"If you're already saying you gon' fuck it up, guess what?" Jaleel grinned knowingly. "You gon' fuck it up. Speak life into your plans. You got it good, LV. Real good. Finding love in a woman like Ivy— someone as good as her, as fine as her, respectfully…" He held his hands up in mock defense. "And on top of that, she's your friend? How do you not see the blessing in that?"

I tilted my head, letting his words sink in.

"That's 'cause you not thinking." He chuckled, shaking his head. "Too busy psyching yourself out, convinced you're gonna mess it all up before even trying. At least try, shit."

Jaleel turned and picked up his ball, his focus sharpened back on the hoop, sinking another shot. Meanwhile, I stayed rooted in place, my thoughts spiraling, struggling to keep up with shooting and everything else crowding my mind

"All I'm saying is," he said, jogging after the ball, "it's never too late to make things right and give it a real try. When you play games, you don't go into it thinking you're gonna lose, right? So stop telling yourself you're gonna lose at love."

"There goes that word again." I pointed at him, my voice low. "Love. Who the hell said anything about love?"

"You didn't have to." Jaleel grinned wide. "It's so fucking obvious, homie." His laughter boomed across the court. "Now, c'mon, let's get back to shooting."

We spent another couple of hours practicing in the gym, the rhythmic thud of basketballs filling the space as my thoughts stayed on what Jaleel had said. Eventually, we hit the locker room to shower and change. After saying goodbye, I climbed into my black car, heading back to my loft.

As the driver navigated through the city, I replayed our conversation over and over. Jaleel's words lingered, each one hitting deeper than I expected.

At a red light, my attention drifted out the window to a playground across the street. The spring air was crisp but warm enough to bring families out to enjoy the day. I spotted a man and woman standing together near the swings, their toddler sitting happily in the bucket seat as they pushed him back and forth.

The man had his arm draped casually over the woman's shoulder, his posture relaxed as he leaned in to kiss her forehead. She smiled up at him before turning her focus back to the child. It was such a simple moment, but something about it made my chest tighten.

Once, seeing something like that would've felt like looking into a prison yard. A wife and kid? Spending free time like that? It always sounded like a life sentence to me. No escape. No freedom.

But as the light turned green and my driver pressed the gas, pulling us away, I found myself craning my neck to steal another glance at them. I wanted to stay in their world a little longer.

Maybe even wanting something like that for myself?

"Oh, shit," I muttered under my breath, my lips curving into a slow, astonished smile. "Wow."

Because in that moment, I realized something I'd never thought I'd admit.

That's exactly what I wanted.

EIGHTEEN

I BALANCED Levi against my chest while trying to single out the key for the house. Moments ago, we'd stepped out of my car—a new luxury SUV I traded my sedan for to better navigate Greene Gardens and make trips to the city with Levi when needed. Like today. I'd taken Levi to his first mommy-and-me activity.

The ladies in the group I'd found online were fascinated by our story, constantly mentioning what a blessing I must be to him. Little did they know he was more of a blessing to me, and I was finally starting to see that.

For May, the weather was beautiful. With summer just a month away, Greene Gardens was living up to its name. Lush green grass, blooming trees, and vibrant flowers created a picturesque view. Outside the house, the scenery felt like an extension of a painting.

With the key in hand, I slid it into the lock, turning it to enter. The moment the door opened, the smell of food hit me.

I paused, wrinkling my brows.

"Hey," Leo called from the kitchen, waving at me.

"Hey…" I stepped inside, blinking through the momentary shock. "What are you doing here?"

He chuckled, turning his attention to a pot on the stove, steam swirling up from it. "I gotta have a reason to be here now?"

I shut the door behind me, heading in his direction.

The last time I saw Leo was a few days ago when he'd dropped Levi back at Greene Gardens after having him for a weekend. Even then, he was acting strange.

Actually, he'd been acting strange ever since his awards ceremony.

That night, I'd noticed something different in how he looked at me. He was attentive, more present, even flirty—like the version of Leo I'd seen with other women he was attracted to. It felt nice, I won't lie, but it was equally confusing.

I dropped Levi's baby bag near the shoe rack as I made my way to Leo. Levi stirred a little in my arms, still drowsy from his nap after our mommy-and-me meetup at a Gymboree in Manhattan.

"Are you... cooking?" I asked, stopping by the kitchen island.

"Yeah." He nodded casually. "My mom shared a chicken stew recipe I figured you'd like."

I arched a brow, rising on the arches of my sneakers to peek into the pot. The sight actually made me smile. "And it looks... edible."

Leo snorted. "Don't play me like that. I grew up in a single mama household. Of course, I know how to cook."

"I grew up in a single mama household and I can barely boil water." I leaned against the counter, watching him.

"Well, your mother is mad laidback. My mama wouldn't let me live under her roof, eating the way I did, without knowing how to cook." He shrugged. "It's a Cheryl thing, I guess."

We stood there for a moment, staring at each other.

Even the way he was looking at me now was different. It wasn't teasing or playful like it usually was. His gaze was softer, more intent, and it did something to me.

Leo always joked about how uptight I was, teasing me for my need for order and structure. But now, there was no trace of that.

"Everything okay?" I asked, adjusting Levi against my shoulder.

"Yeah, everything's good." He smiled. "Why?"

I narrowed my eyes at him. "Because you're acting weird."

"Damn." He laughed softly, shaking his head. "A man can't just cook for you?"

"You cooked specifically for me?"

"Yeah." He shrugged, as if it were no big deal.

I blinked a few times, my head tilting slightly. "First the Woman Crush Wednesday post a few days ago, and now this?"

He licked his lips, offering a small smirk. "Yeah."

I didn't know what to make of this shift. Since the night I tried to talk to him—the night he was getting ready to meet up with Vanessa, his friend-with-benefits—he'd been guarded. Closed off.

After that, I decided to mirror his energy. We'd hooked up twice, and he clearly didn't want to discuss it, so I wasn't going to lose sleep over it. When he told me he was moving back to his loft in the city, I forced myself to accept it. I shut down emotionally and made Levi my only priority.

But now?

As much as I tried to stay closed off, I couldn't ignore the pull I felt. The way he was looking at me, cooking for me, posting about me.

It made me wonder if Leo felt it too.

This unexplainable pull.

This... possibility.

I cleared my throat, quickly dismissing the swirling thoughts in my head. Peeking down at Levi, still peacefully asleep, I refocused on Leo. "I'm going to walk him to his nursery, set him down, and freshen up in my room."

"Cool." He nodded. "The food will be ready whenever you're ready."

As I walked away, I glanced back toward the kitchen.

He was cooking... for me.

The whole thing was perplexing.

After laying Levi in his crib, I only took off his jacket before gently covering him with a lightweight blanket. I grabbed the baby monitor on my way out, closing the nursery door softly behind me.

As I headed to my room, I turned the monitor on, keeping my eyes on the screen. Lifting my attention just in time to avoid bumping into the doorway, I did a double take as I stepped inside my room.

I suppressed a laugh, my jaw slacked as I stared at what was before me.

Red roses. Made out of LEGOs.

My dresser was covered in vases filled with intricately crafted Lego roses.

There were so many I couldn't begin to count.

I approached the dresser, marveling at the plastic roses. The detail in them was insane.

"I had no idea such a thing existed," I murmured to myself.

"Neither did I," Leo said from behind me.

I turned quickly, startled to find him standing there, holding another vase of Lego roses in his hands.

It was... adorable. The sight of all those roses filling my dresser, the time it must have taken to put them together—it made my heart swell.

"Leo, what the—" I shook my head, a laugh escaping me. "What is happening right now?"

He walked into the room, setting the larger vase he was holding beside the others on my dresser.

Before I could fully process it, he closed the space between us. His hand cupped my chin, gently turning my face to meet his gaze.

His eyes were locked on mine, softer than I'd ever seen them, but still carrying a playful glint. Yet, beneath that playfulness, there was something serious.

"I'm sorry," he said, his voice low and steady. "I'm so sorry for how I acted last month after we got physical. It was childish and stupid. I couldn't make sense of what was happening between us, and I didn't want to fuck anything up if we continued to take things further."

"And what's happening now?" I asked, my voice barely above a whisper as I glanced between him and the roses on the dresser. "What's all of this?"

Leo licked his lips slowly, his expression growing more resolute.

"You being here, cooking…" I gestured toward the Lego roses. "Filling my room with these. What's happening right now?"

"I caught feelings for you, Ivy," he admitted. "Big feelings. Colossal."

My brows shot up.

"I caught feelings for you that I never knew were there until we uncovered them." He took both my hands in his, stepping even closer. "I didn't know how to process what happened between us the first night. But when I couldn't stop thinking about you—even when I tried to hang out with Vanessa the way we used to—I realized that night wasn't just a hookup. It meant something."

I swallowed hard, nodding as he continued.

"That was just a hunch until the second time. That time… things felt different for me. Real."

"They felt different for me too," I admitted, my voice trembling. "And I haven't been able to figure out why. We've known each other for years, Leo, and not once have we seen each other like that. I don't know. Maybe it's all this stuff we've been through together these past few months."

"But what if it's not?" His thumb gently stroked the back of my hand. "What if it's something more? Something real? Something we didn't notice before because we didn't allow ourselves to?"

I shook my head, glancing away, overwhelmed by the weight of his words.

"It's crazy, I know." He chuckled softly. "It feels crazy to me too. But it feels right at the same time."

I studied him, my heart racing as I watched the rise and fall of his chest.

This was unreal.

Leo and I had been opposites from the start. We wouldn't have even been friends if not for our mutual friends. But now... now it was like we couldn't ignore whatever was building between us.

His gaze dropped to my lips, and I scoffed. "Why are you looking at me like you want to kiss me?"

He cradled my face with both hands, his touch warm and steady.

"Because I wanna kiss you," he said.

"An interested Leo seems to be a more honest and forthcoming Leo." A smile tugged at my lips. "I'm not used to that."

His fingers brushed along the edge of my jaw, then buried themselves in my hair. His simple, *"Mm-hmm,"* was all the warning I got before his lips claimed mine.

I exhaled sharply against him, my body instinctively closing the distance between us. My hands ran up his back, my fingertips pressing into his warm skin as he lowered his tall frame to deepen the kiss.

In one fluid motion, I was in his arms, and a second later, he was walking me to the bed.

It didn't take long for us to shed layers, our movements eager but deliberate. His hands moved quickly, helping me out of my tee and jeans before stripping out of his own clothes with just as much urgency.

When he stood at the foot of the bed, sliding his boxers down, I couldn't resist crawling toward him. My hands wrapped around his dick, and without hesitation, I lowered my mouth to the tip, tasting him.

"Shit," he groaned, his voice husky and weighted with need. "Damn."

The way he stiffened against the roof of my mouth sent a rush of heat through me. Slowly, I worked him, sucking him in and letting him slide out with intentional tension. His hand found its way to my hair, holding my strands in a firm but gentle grasp.

"Fuck," he whispered, his breath hitching. His head dropped

back, and he gave up trying to stifle his groans. "What *can't* you do, baby? *Mmm...*"

His patience wore thin after a few moments. With a strained groan, he pulled me away and eased me back onto the bed.

I gasped softly, inhaling his exhale as he guided himself between my thighs. The sensation of him sliding into my wet heat sent a ripple of anticipation through me.

The first time we did this, it had been a whirlwind—intense, shocking, and like releasing something pent up inside both of us. The second time was natural, like it had been waiting to happen all along.

This time? It felt familiar.

Each stroke was trained, slow, and unhurried. His lips never left mine, our breaths mingling as he pushed deeper. He lifted one of my legs, angling me so perfectly I couldn't help but arch my back.

"God, I've missed you," he murmured, his words hot against my lips. He pecked my mouth softly, his hips rolling deeper.

I giggled, breathless. "You haven't had me enough to miss me."

"Oh, baby," he growled, his voice dropping an octave. "The two times were more than enough. Trust me."

Our attempts to keep quiet dissolved with every thrust. The intensity built between us, the friction both figurative and literal. He slipped his hand beneath me, gripping my ass to open me more, taking me fully, completely.

And there was so much to take.

Leo wasn't shy, and God hadn't held back when blessing him.

The way we moved together, my body meeting his strokes, felt surreal. What kind of alternate universe had we stumbled into?

"You feel like you're mine," he rasped, his movements slowing to a maddening pace. His words sent a shiver down my spine. "And only mine."

My mind was spinning, lost in a haze of ecstasy.

"Are you mine, Ivy?"

"*Mmm...*" I smiled lazily, teasing. "Possessive much?"

"When you feel like this around me?" His hips circled, eliciting a sharp gasp from me. "Hell fucking yeah."

"*Mmm*, Leo." My voice was shaky, caught between laughter and moans. "Keep doing that."

"Oh, I will." His thrusts gained speed, each one more precise than the last. "I'll keep doing it every day if you want me to."

I giggled, then moaned again, my body arching into his.

"Can I do this to you every day, Ivy?" he groaned, his voice thick with need. "Can it be me and only me doing whatever you want me to do to you?"

My hand smoothed over his back, sliding to his firm backside, pushing him even deeper.

"Can I, Ivy?"

"I'll tell you whatever you want me to say right now," I whispered, sucking in a sharp breath through my teeth.

"I want the truth," he murmured, gripping me tighter, angling me to take him even more.

"Oooh, God!"

"I could make you feel like this all the time." His lips traveled from my ear to my cheek, stopping at my chin. "I could make your body do more than this."

I chuckled weakly, my laugh trembling. "You're sounding real toxic right now delivering good dick and sweet promises—"

"I love you," he panted suddenly.

And that made me level my head. "What?"

He paused everything, his movements coming to a halt as he stared at me, our bodies still connected.

"You don't have to say it back," he assured me, his chest heaving with every breath. "I just... I do."

"Oh, my God." My eyes widened. "Leo!"

"*Shh*," he murmured, brushing his lips against mine as he resumed his strokes, slow and purposeful. "You don't have to say it back. Just come with me." He nodded slowly. "Come with me."

There was something in the way he said it—*I love you*—that

resonated deeply. It wasn't a fleeting declaration born out of the heat of the moment. It was raw and honest, wrapped in sincerity, vulnerability, and a dash of uncertainty.

If I thought I was feeling good before, hearing those words amplified everything. I was fully present, my senses heightened, every nerve ending tuned to him.

He took my hands, threading his fingers through mine, and held them out to the sides. His movements were steady, rhythmic, as his gaze locked on mine.

Leo didn't just make love to me—he consumed me. His body spoke to mine, his strokes precise, unraveling every defense I had. My jaw went slack, my vision blurred, and tears stung my eyes, distorting the view of his face.

"Yes," he whispered, picking up speed. "Come with me, baby. Oh, God, Ivy, come with me just like that."

And I did. Completely.

The sensation coursing through me was overwhelming. My body surrendered, moving in perfect harmony with his. I gripped his hands tightly, holding on as though my life depended on it. My entire world narrowed to the pulsing rhythm between us.

The sounds we made—the wet slaps of skin, the creak of the bed, and our mingled breaths—drowned out everything else. I let go of his hands, clutching his back as the intensity overtook me.

Leo groaned deeply, his thrusts slowing, each one a purposeful, final push. Together, we unraveled, collapsing into a shared breathless silence.

* * *

Leo's hand skimmed down my thigh, his fingers dancing lightly over my skin before trailing back up. His lips didn't give mine a moment of reprieve, stealing kiss after kiss as though he'd never get enough.

I tried to turn my head away, laughing through my protests, but he only shifted closer, pressing kisses along my neck.

"Oh, my God." I giggled, my voice breathless. "Will I ever breathe my own air again?"

"Nope," he said against my mouth, his grin evident in his tone. He tugged me closer by the thigh, positioning himself between my legs again.

The sun had risen, marking a new day, but we hadn't gotten much sleep. Between devouring the meal Leo had made and tending to Levi throughout the night, every moment in between was spent tangled together.

Now, lying beneath him in one of his oversized tees, with him completely bare against me, I could feel his fingers slipping between my thighs.

"*Mmm*," I moaned softly as his fingers found their mark, circling my clit with firm, concentrated strokes. I spread my legs wider, giving him better access.

"Your touch is insane," I whispered, my body arching into him.

"*Mm-hmm*," he murmured, his voice a velvet rasp. "I'm very good with my hands and other parts of me as you know."

He proved his point by sliding his tongue into my mouth, his rhythm with his fingers perfectly synced to the kiss.

To say I could get used to this would be an understatement. It had only been 24 hours since we'd acknowledged this undeniable pull between us, but already it felt like home.

Kendra's journal sat open on the nightstand beside us, turned to the page where she detailed the baby names she and Tyrell had chosen. Leo and I planned to call the estate lawyer that morning to make Levi's name official, but Leo had other priorities.

Not that I was complaining.

My hips moved instinctively to the rhythm of his fingers, my body attuned to his every touch. I ran my hand up the back of his head, smoothing my fingers over his fade.

I'd never known intimacy like this.

We'd spent years convinced we weren't right for each other, that we couldn't work. But these past few months—and especially these last 24 hours—had told an entirely different story.

"I swear," he breathed, his voice thick with emotion, "every moment with you feels like I'm exactly where I'm supposed to be."

His words sent a shiver through me, my body rolling against his hand as the pressure built steadily.

"You know I don't just want right now with you, right?" he whispered, his lips brushing my ear as he pressed harder against my clit. "I want right now..."

"Oooh, Leo."

"... and every tomorrow we can have together," he finished, his voice low and dripping with intent.

"You gotta stop telling me shit like this when you're making me come," I whined, my voice a breathless whisper.

He smirked, brushing his lips against mine. "You gonna let me be the best part of your day, then?"

"*Mmm*," I hummed, unable to form coherent words.

"Every day, no matter what?"

"I'm right there," I panted, gripping his shoulders as his lips grazed mine again.

"Let me taste and see," he replied, his grin devilish. He slid down my body, his face disappearing between my thighs.

The swirl of his tongue had me pressing into him. I let out a shaky breath, one hand fisting the sheets while the other gripped the back of his head. He groaned into me, the vibration sending ripples through my body as he sucked and licked with unrelenting precision.

My hips bucked off the bed involuntarily, and his large hand pressed firmly against my stomach, grounding me.

"Leo," I whispered, my voice shaking as I teetered on the edge.

He finished me off with expert ease, leaving me utterly boneless and gasping for air. As my body calmed, he placed two kisses on my sensitive center before trailing back up my body.

Leo braced himself above me, arms strong on either side, and guided himself inside, moving with a concentrated, slow rhythm that made my toes curl.

Just as I closed my eyes to let the sensations take me over, we heard Levi stirring in his crib, followed shortly by his cries.

Leo paused, his forehead resting against mine as he let out a soft laugh. "Perfect timing."

He kissed me once more and whispered, "I'll get him."

"No." I pressed a quick peck to his lips. "I'll get him. You have no clothes on, and you have me all over your mouth."

He licked his lips and smirked. "I like you all over my mouth."

I giggled, nudging him off gently before slipping on my robe and heading to the nursery.

Levi's cries quieted the moment I scooped him up.

"Hey cutie," I cooed, smiling at him. "How was your sleep?"

His wide, gummy smile melted me, as it always did.

"Good, then?" I asked, smiling even wider in return.

As I held him, I couldn't help but reflect on the whirlwind of changes in my life. Reading Kendra's journal had given me clarity, helping me see the blessings I never realized were all around me. I thought I had everything figured out before she passed, but now? I realized I was only just beginning to understand what mattered.

When I walked back into the room, Levi tucked against my chest, Leo had slipped into basketball shorts and a tee.

"I got him," Leo said, stepping toward me and holding out his hands. "Go freshen up."

He winked, making me laugh as I handed Levi over.

In the en suite, I stared at my reflection, brushing my teeth and shaking my head at how much my life had changed. A house in Greene Gardens. Leo. Levi. It was all so unexpected, but somehow, it felt right.

I was finishing up when Leo stepped into the bathroom. Levi was cradled effortlessly in his arms, drinking his bottle contentedly.

"I'm heading downstairs to put something together to eat," he said casually.

I turned to face him, smiling at the sight. "You want me to take the baby?"

"Nah," he replied, shaking his head. "You finish up here."

He leaned in for a kiss, and I met him halfway, our lips lingering for a moment before he pulled back, smiling softly.

"Leo."

"*Hmm?*" he asked, turning back to look at me.

There he stood—big, confident, and undeniably handsome—holding Levi like it was the most natural thing in the world. The sight made my heart ache in the best way.

"I love you too," I said, my voice quiet but sure.

A smile spread across his face, wide and genuine. He nodded, his eyes warm as they met mine. "I know."

I laughed, shaking my head at his confidence.

"Come down when you're done," he said, turning to leave. "Take your time."

As he walked out of the bathroom, I stood there, the smile on my face refusing to fade.

This alternate universe, this unexpected life? It was everything I never knew I wanted. And I had no intention of leaving it behind.

6 MONTHS LATER...

LEO

I STOOD over a mountain of green peppers, sorting through each one in search of the perfect ones for my mother's stew recipe. Ivy and I had decided to make it together, a recipe she'd been wanting to try ever since my mom walked her through it on FaceTime.

I was at the Greene Gardens Market, the only market in the village. It was my third visit here. My first time was when my agent, Simeon, asked me to check on the display of apples from his parents' farm, which supplied produce to the market. My second visit was less about errands and more about desperation when Levi spiked a high fever, and his doctor suggested cooling gel pads to help bring his temperature down. Those pads worked wonders, even if they didn't ease his frustration one bit.

That night had been one of the hardest for Ivy and me since moving in together.

Levi's cries echoed through the house, pulling me from a deep sleep. He'd been fussy and feverish all day, likely due to teething, according to his doctor. Ivy and I had been working in shifts, taking turns rocking him back to sleep. It was her turn now.

Since the night we made love in her room, I'd started sleeping in Ivy's bed. At first, it was just practical—the master bedroom had the attached en suite and was closer to Levi's nursery. But over time, it became impossible to sleep anywhere else when I knew the woman I loved was just down the hall. Ivy liked to joke that I only went back to my own room to "play with Legos," and she wasn't entirely wrong.

Levi's cries softened as Ivy reached his room, but the whining didn't stop completely. I was exhausted, having returned home late after a game the night prior. But the sound of Ivy's soft humming through the baby monitor tugged at me.

I pulled myself out of bed and headed to the nursery because that's what good boyfriends and godfathers do.

When I entered, Ivy was sitting in the rocker, holding Levi against her chest and pressing a teething ring to his gums. Her eyes were heavy with exhaustion, and her head dropped back slightly between her shoulders as she bounced him gently.

I approached, placing a hand against Levi's forehead. Warm, but not as bad as earlier.

Yawning, I grabbed the infant pain medicine off the dresser, measured out the dosage, and brought it to her. She stood from her seat on the rocker to meet me by the dresser.

"Angle his head a little," I said, my voice rough with sleep.

She adjusted Levi, letting me carefully pour the medicine into his mouth. He swallowed it down without a fight.

Ivy yawned as she patted Levi's back, her head falling forward against me. I wrapped my arms around both of them, pressing a kiss to the top of her head.

"Thank you," she whispered, her voice soft.

I leaned my head against hers, my hand rubbing small circles on her back. "Thank you, too."

Levi's cries quieted into soft, even breaths. He was finally asleep again.

The two of us had found our rhythm in this house, learning to work together to care for Levi so neither of us carried the burden alone. It wasn't always easy, but it had been worth it. And since we'd embraced the relationship growing between us, things felt even more natural.

Now, standing in the market on my third trip here, everything about this little village had become familiar.

"Leo Vanguard?" a voice called from behind me.

I turned to see a pretty, brown-skinned woman approaching with a shopping cart and a bright smile.

"Hey!" she greeted warmly. "What's up?"

I smiled back. "Just shopping... for groceries. You?"

She laughed, looking genuinely excited. "I'm Alexis."

"Nice to meet you, Alexis."

"I don't usually do this," she admitted, waving a hand. "I know it's, like, a rule not to bother celebrities, but I'm just way too hype to see another famous face out here." Her eyes darted around before landing on someone behind me. "Keith!" she shouted, motioning toward him. "Keith, look who it is!"

I snickered to myself, already turning toward the direction of her gesture.

Coming toward us was none other than *the* Keith Aaron, the rapper whose career had been exploding recently, especially after one of his songs was featured in a major movie.

"Oh, shit," I said, adjusting the basket in my arm to hold my fist out for him to bump, which he did. "You out here?"

He laughed, then pointed at the woman. "Yeah, because of my girl. *You* out here?"

"Yeah." I smiled. "I live out here."

Keith's brows shot up. "Word?"

"See?" The woman bumped her shoulder with him. "One of the NBA's hottest players calls Greene Gardens home. Take that."

I chuckled.

"She's been trying to get me out here..." Keith's eyes moved around the market. "I'm thinking it over. It's beautiful."

"Very beautiful," I added.

"But, it ain't Manhattan," Keith added. "Feel me?"

"Oh, I feel you." I laughed. "That's why I've gotten involved with some community initiatives. The businesses around Manhattan are what make it appealing. If Greene Gardens gets some of those businesses to set up locations out here, it could be Manhattan 2.0."

"Hmph," Keith huffed.

"They got a business improvement district out here," I informed. "They hold meetings every month downtown, giving locals an opportunity to participate in discussions on how to attract more businesses and visitors with special events and beautification projects, man..." I nodded. "They got some real big plans for Greene Gardens. Don't sleep on it."

"Thank you." Alexis grunted. "That's exactly what I've been trying to tell his hard-headed ass."

Keith slapped her on the ass, and I snorted a laugh. He pointed at her next. "You *shhh.*"

"I'm working with them to develop a local athletic facility so I can have a basketball court, gymnasiums, and sports complex to train in, so I don't have to go all the way out to the city." I shrugged. "Home is what you make it. Feel me?"

"*I* feel you," Alexis said with a nod. "Anyway, we won't hold you. I just needed to make a damn point to this guy."

Keith kissed his teeth while turning to me to hold his hand out for a dap. "Pleasure meeting you, Leo."

"Man, likewise," I replied, accepting his dap. "*Between the Lines* is one of my favorite albums."

Keith pressed his hand to his chest and nodded. "That means a lot, for real."

"It was good meeting you too, Leo." Alexis smiled. "I'll see you around."

"Yes, you will," I replied with a smile as they walked off.

I spent a little more time at the market, selecting the rest of the ingredients I needed, then took them to the register to check out.

I had finished shopping and was back in my brand-new SUV, which I'd gotten after selling my city loft and deciding to live in

Greene Gardens full-time. The decision became an easy one once I realized that home was wherever Ivy and Levi were… which was kind of difficult to explain to my friend-with-benefits, Vanessa.

"So, y'all finally stopped lying to yourselves?" Vanessa asked me over coffee. "Or are you finally done lying to me?"

I'd invited her to a café in Brooklyn shortly after my night back in Greene Gardens with Ivy. Though Ivy had never questioned what being involved with her meant for me and Vanessa, I thought it was time to end whatever thing Vanessa and I had. It was the moral thing to do for all of us.

"I was never lying to you," I explained. "I honestly never saw Ivy like that until after we moved out to Greene Gardens."

Vanessa sucked her teeth loudly, looking off and shaking her head. "I knew something was up when we stopped having sex months ago, so…" Her arms had been in a tight fold from the time she arrived, and I told her my plans to move back to Greene Gardens.

Vanessa and I hadn't seen each other much since I returned to Manhattan. Hadn't slept together since Ivy and my first hookup. I enjoyed Vanessa's company, but we were never really for each other. We had very little in common besides sex.

"You know I moved out to Manhattan for you, right?" She laughed cynically. "Packed up all my shit and moved out here from Atlanta for a guy who wouldn't even give me the title of girlfriend." Her arms came out of their fold so she could point at me. "I don't know why you asked me here to tell me this when we were never together, right? We were just fucking, right?"

I looked around me, then leaned in. "Can you please keep your voice down?"

"So what?" she continued. "You're gonna marry her now?"

I jerked my head back, the question unexpected.

I honestly hadn't considered the idea of marriage until that moment. And the idea didn't make me recoil in the least. The idea actually made a smile pull at one corner of my mouth as I imagined Ivy and me in a role like husband and wife.

She'd make a damn good wife. That would be a really good win for me, actually.

After too long of a silence between us—me staring out into the distance, spending a little too long on the idea of marriage with Ivy—Vanessa released an audible exhale.

"You know what, whatever." She pushed her chair back, the legs scraping loudly against the floor. "Good luck. I hope you live happily ever after with the friend I knew your ass loved from the very first time you introduced me to her short ass. I hope you two have a good fucking life."

Vanessa snatched up her designer bag from the back of her chair.

"By the way," Vanessa added, pushing her arm through the straps of her bag. She leaned in close enough for her words to sting. "I've been fucking your teammate, the rookie Xavien, for the past year, and I'm glad I was smart enough to do it."

My brows shot up. "Excuse me?"

"See you around," she said, walking off. "Asshole."

It didn't feel good knowing Vanessa felt that way after everything. It didn't feel good to know I was sleeping with the same woman who was sleeping with someone I knew, either. But that was life then, and this was my life now. I would do exactly what Vanessa wished me to do—have a good life. A damn good one.

Before starting up my SUV to head home, I called Ivy to let her know I was on my way back.

"Hey," she said into the phone, her voice instantly putting a smile on my face. "You get everything?"

"I did," I replied, nodding to myself. "Even ran into Keith Aaron at the market."

"The rapper?"

"Yeah. He was there with his girl."

"Dope."

"I'll be home soon," I told her. "You got everything set up and ready to start?"

"You know I do."

I chuckled softly.

Things with Ivy had been good. It didn't take long for me to ask her what we were doing. I wanted a relationship the moment I sat at my desk putting together a dozen of tiny Lego roses... which she still has and loves.

Never in a million years would I have guessed that the woman who would steal my heart in such an unpredictable way had been right under my nose the whole time. Ivy was everything I needed. The balance to my life that made everything seem possible.

We started this journey all messed up in the head—given a baby we had no experience with, our plans for life turned upside down. But now? I was so settled in this new life, my old one didn't even cross my mind. I didn't miss it, not a little bit.

I was grateful for the storm that came in and cleared out what I thought I wanted.

Though it still hurt most days to remember my best friend was gone—and the one-year anniversary of his passing was slowly approaching—what his loss helped me gain made up for it in small but meaningful ways. My life felt like mine again, and I had two people waiting for me at home who I loved with all my heart.

Greene Gardens finally felt like home.

Happiness felt good when it was real.

And now, I was on my way home to the love of my life.

Life was definitely good—and it was just getting started.

* * *

IVY

I sat at my desk, grinning from ear to ear as my eyes stayed glued to one of my computer screens.

I was watching a post-game interview with one of the journalists from *Free-Throw Nation* interviewing Leo after his game against the Atlanta Hawks the night before.

"Leo, congratulations on that spectacular performance tonight," the interviewer, Scott Sanders, said, enthusiasm ringing in his voice. He was one of our newest hires at *Free-Throw Nation*, but his passion for the game made him a great fit. "How does it feel to come away with such a decisive win?"

"Thanks, man," Leo replied, running a hand down his face to wipe away the sweat. "It feels amazing, honestly. The team really pulled together tonight—everyone was firing on all cylinders. We've got a plan this season, and we're just out here working it."

"Yes, you all are," Scott added.

"You know, it's games like these that remind us why we work so hard every day," Leo said between breaths. "My team and I have been training together since before pre-training, so we all share this win tonight."

"Absolutely," Scott nodded.

Some days, I missed being out on the court. Inhaling the energy in the arena, hearing the squeak of sneakers on the hardwood—it all felt like home once. But life now? Life was the perfect opposite. There was so much to love now, especially the guy getting interviewed on screen.

"It was a team effort, for sure," Scott continued. "Now, can you walk us through that final play? What was going through your mind?"

Leo laughed. "Well, we had the play set up during the timeout, and I knew I had to create some space to either take the shot..." He gestured with his hands. "Or find an open man. The defense bit on the fake, and that split second was all we needed, baby. Just focused on executing what we've practiced. What we've *been* practicing."

"Impressive as always," Scott smiled. "So, Leo, how does someone like Leo Vanguard celebrate after a win like this?"

Leo chuckled, pressing a hand to his chest. "Well, Scott, tonight's plan is pretty simple: I'm about to go home, kiss my amazing godson goodnight if he's still up, and then cuddle up next to my girl."

"Oh, my God." I shook my head while smiling. "He did not have to say that!"

Scott chuckled.

"She's one of my favorite people in the world, and honestly, the greatest sports journalist to ever do it—no offense," Leo said during his interview, shooting Scott a playful look.

Scott laughed, clearly enjoying the banter. "None taken. I'm in good company since we both work at the same network."

I rolled my eyes at the screen and kissed my teeth. "Scott, don't give that man rope, please."

"Good company you are definitely in," Leo added, patting Scott on the back. Then, looking directly into the camera, he said with a grin, "Be home soon, Ivy League."

I scoffed, my grin widening as I hit the button to minimize the video frame. "He can be such an attention whore."

An attention whore that I loved. And since he's started whispering his little nickname for me into my ear while buried very deeply inside of me, I didn't hate it as much anymore.

A lot had changed since that fateful day I returned home to find Leo in the kitchen cooking and a slew of roses made out of LEGOs in my bedroom. It's literally been amazing—both romantically and professionally—two areas of my life I didn't think could experience any kind of amazing-ness after unexpectedly becoming Levi's guardian.

The *Free-Throw Nation* column I thought was a weak consolation prize for what I really wanted—an anchor position at the network— was booming and doing far better than I ever expected. My column was referenced by the who's who in sports media, constantly cited for insightful commentary and quoted in newscasts. It got to the point where I felt a little pressure every time I typed my random thoughts, but it was the best kind of pressure.

My YouTube channel had grown beyond my wildest dreams, so much so that the network gave me a separate vlogging channel just for my very random sports commentary. I was being paid to be myself, something I didn't think was possible.

And because my visibility increased professionally, my personal life had become a story in itself. People were fascinated by the way Leo and I became guardians of Levi. Our journey caught the attention of brands that now sent us sponsorship offers because of our engaging content—and our relationship.

A relationship Leo made public every chance he got.

Which, honestly, I didn't mind at all.

Life was so different now. It was unlike anyone's I knew. It was, honestly... great.

I logged into my social media account, preparing to go live on *Free-Throw Nation's* account. I was scheduled to talk about last night's game—Ballers versus Hawks—and now that I knew about Leo's final comments during his interview, I was certain the viewers would bring it up.

Leo never missed a chance to show his affection, whether it was verbal or physical. Since moving back to Greene Gardens, he'd become a full-on family man. He went to the games, then came straight home. There was very little partying or clubbing for Leo Vanguard these days. Watching him keep his promise to prioritize family was one of the sexiest things I'd ever witnessed.

Once everything was set up, I pressed the red circle to go live, running my fingers through my hair before gathering it into a messy bun.

These days, I didn't bother spending hours perfecting my appearance for casual live streams. Sure, for in-person events or high-profile outings, I'd put in the effort, but my fans loved me as I was—even preferred it. Knowing that took a lot of the stress out of always needing to look "on point."

"Hey, everyone, Ivy here," I said to the camera, smiling brightly. "Coming to you live from my office, as always." I giggled. "With the freshest takes from last night's electric game! Thank you for tuning in, wherever in the world you're tuning in from. Let's get into the excitement of the hardwood, are you ready?"

Comments immediately started streaming in as I clicked through my notes, smiling at the familiar buzz of engagement.

I didn't think much about my life before Levi anymore. When I missed that life, it was only because I missed Kendra. Those feelings hadn't subsided, but I'd learned how to cope with them. Sometimes, a random social media post would pop up and send me into uncontrollable tears. Other times, I'd get the urge to call her before remembering I couldn't.

There was even a voicemail she'd left me years ago that I still listened to when missing her felt unbearable. It helped.

"First off," I said, glancing at the camera. "Can we *please* talk about that incredible performance from the Bronx Ballers last night? And I know someone here is going to say I'm biased, but—" I held up a finger—"you can't deny they truly brought their A-game, okay? But one player really stood out. Of course, I'm talking about Leo Vanguard." I winked. "His strategic plays and unstoppable energy were key to clinching that win. So, let's break down some of those highlight moments!"

Leo didn't waste any time asking me what we were doing when he moved back to Greene Gardens.

"You want a relationship?" I asked one night over bowls of cereal we were sharing in the middle of the night.

We'd taken a break from having sex, which we'd been doing almost every hour since his return. A bowl of cereal and an island between us was the only thing keeping us apart.

"Don't you?" he replied, shoveling a spoonful of cereal into his mouth. "I thought women preferred that."

I snorted. "I'm fine either way."

Leo dropped his spoon into his bowl and looked at me. "Look, woman, do you want to be my girlfriend or nah?"

Of course, I said yes.

And it's been one of the best decisions I've ever made.

"Looking at the third quarter," I started, easing back into the live stream after composing myself. "Leo made a game-changing steal followed by a fast-break dunk that sent the crowd into a frenzy. This moment was pivotal, shifting the momentum in favor of the Ballers."

Leo had been working hard. The season had just started, but his determination to lead his team to the championship was palpable. I believed in him and his vision, and I was confident he and his team could achieve it.

I was proud of him—proud of us, too. Somehow, we'd figured this thing out, navigating life together in a way that worked. Levi had a balanced schedule with both of us chipping in, plus support from Kendra's parents, Tyrell's mom, and our own mothers. It truly was taking a village, and yet, there were still days when it felt over-whelming. I didn't know how people did it alone, but I had nothing but admiration for those who managed it.

Grief counseling had become my regular reason to leave Greene Gardens. My connection with Rylee had grown, and she was now someone I considered a close friend. She was a steady light in those moments when Kendra's absence felt like a shadow threatening to engulf me.

"Leo's role as a team leader was more apparent than ever last night, y'all," I continued, glancing back at my notes. "Watching him communicate on the court, set up plays, and rally his team was like attending a masterclass in basketball leadership. His performance last night is a testament to his hard work and dedication, both on and off the court."

The words had barely left my mouth when the office door swung open.

"Yo..." Leo called, pointing at me, then at himself. "It's time to pay up." He winked. "You and me. The bed upstairs, right now. Everything off."

I widened my eyes at him, caught between surprise and amusement.

"Don't give me that look," he added with a smirk, his tone teas-ing. "You lost the bet when you said I couldn't pass as much as I shot in last night's game. Well, I proved you wrong, and now it's time to pay up and for you to do that thing I like. So, please may we head up to the bed upstairs? No clothes though. I'll even give you a massage first... even though you lost the bet."

I gestured at my phone's camera with my eyes, hoping he'd catch the hint.

"Oh, shit!" His hand flew to his mouth in horror. "Are you hosting a live right now?"

I squeezed my eyes shut, covering my face as I started laughing.

Unfazed, Leo stepped into the room and leaned down to peer directly into the camera.

"What up, y'all?" he greeted, flashing a wide grin.

The comments exploded, streaming in faster than I could read them.

"What my lady on here talking about?" Leo asked, looking between me and the screen.

I snorted.

"Oh, me?" He grinned, his gaze shifting to me. "You're talking about me?"

"I am."

"Good things?"

I winked. "Great things."

"Last night's game?" he whispered.

"*Mm-hmm,*" I replied, trying not to laugh. "I watched the post-game interview, by the way." I pinched his arm, making him laugh. "You better stop calling me that."

He leaned in and pressed a kiss to my neck, his voice low against my skin. "I thought I was starting to make you love it."

"Get out," I whispered, biting back a smile.

"I'm gonna make you love it," he murmured with a smirk.

"I'd love to see it," I mumbled, shaking my head.

"I'm gonna check on Levi," he said, leaving a soft kiss on my lips that made me blush. "And I'll be watching your live from the bed... where I want you after you're done."

"You better leave," I whispered.

Leo snickered as he walked to the door, turning back to address my viewers. "Y'all treat her well. Peace."

I couldn't help but giggle, shaking my head as I ran a hand along the side of my face.

I swear, this is exactly why my new sports editor insisted I record my commentary videos from home. This wasn't the first time Leo had interrupted one of my lives, and my interruptions during his live streams had become equally common. Those moments were what led to our sponsorships and brand deals with lifestyle and baby product companies.

As much as I pretended to be annoyed, I secretly loved it.

"*Psst*," I heard from the office door.

I glanced over to see him winking at me.

"I'm serious about that bed, Pressman." He smirked. "And that massage."

"Go!" I shouted, laughing as he backed out of the room.

Before closing the door, he opened it again to say, "I love you."

A smile broke across my face. "I love you too."

I bit my bottom lip, trying to refocus on the camera.

"I'm sorry, y'all." I giggled nervously, throwing my hands in the air. "As you already know, every so often, you're gonna spot a Baller around here." I smiled at the flood of mushy responses pouring in. "All right, that's enough of those comments. Let's get back to it. Where was I?"

After finishing the recording and ending the live, I pushed my office chair back and stood to my feet en route to bed.

The night was still early, just after 9 p.m. Leo and I had dinner earlier—food we'd prepared together, like we often did now.

I could already predict that someone had recorded that live and it would end up on a sports blog or in a feed online. That was just how it went these days.

When I opened the master bedroom door—a room that was once only mine but was now ours—Leo looked up from where he was reclined on the bed.

"I love a woman who follows orders," he teased, sitting up and setting his phone beside him. "Great live, as always."

"Thank you." I smiled, gesturing toward Levi's nursery. "Was he still sleeping when you checked in on him?"

"Like a log," Leo replied, motioning for me to come to him.

I didn't hesitate, climbing onto the bed and straddling him, my legs draped on either side of his hips.

"I'm sorry I interrupted your live," he said, his hands running up and down my thighs, his touch warm and familiar.

I trailed my fingers up his bare chest, stopping at his shoulders. "They loved it. Like always."

Leaning forward, I pressed my lips to his, parting them just enough to slide my tongue against his. The kiss was slow and deep, leaving us both moaning into each other as his body melted into mine.

He quickly flipped us over, pressing me into the bed beneath him, his weight grounding me in the best way.

"So, how are you planning to pay up tonight?" he asked, his lips tracing kisses along my neck. "It's your choice, baby... even though you lost the bet. But I can be a gentleman about it."

"*Mmm*," I hummed, arching into his touch. "I'll do whatever you want me to do. Just tell me. I always make good on my bets."

"My girl."

I snickered softly as he captured my lips again, his kiss stealing my breath and making my heart race.

My life was now the complete opposite of what I once thought I wanted. The idea of being in a relationship and having a baby used to fill me with so much anxiety that I swore it could never be for me.

I was so worried when Kendra told me she was having a baby, concerned about how much her life—and mine by extension—would change.

And it did change... for the better.

Bittersweet, yet undeniably better.

THE END.

final words

Dear Reader,

Thank you so much for picking up *Raising Love*! I really hope you found the ending as fulfilling as I did when I wrote it. This story launches my newest setting, Greene Gardens, which I've been eager to share with you. It's a little world built within another world from a previous series.

In the Character Cameo section mentioned earlier, you'll find details about the side characters who pop up in *Raising Love*. While Bryant Greene, the billionaire behind Greene Gardens, doesn't feature in this book, I've included his story from *Greed* (book three in the Love is Cure, Vol. 1 – Vices & Virtues series) so you can discover the origins of Greene Gardens.

If you enjoyed *Raising Love*, I'd love for you to explore more friends-to-lovers stories I've written; it's a trope I adore both writing and reading. Titles like *Girl Code, So This is Love, Just Friends*, and *Last Comes Love* are just a few I'd recommend.

Thanks again for reading. If this was your first book by me, I hope you consider yourself a Brookelynite now! And to all my longtime readers, your support inspires me daily and fuels my passion for storytelling. Thank you for everything!

See you at the end of my next book!

Love always,
Brookelyn

character cameos

In the order they appeared or were mentioned in Raising Love. Type the following link in your browser to find links to all titles listed below: (https://bit.ly/3QdG4c6)

Bryant Greene

GREED

Home Before Midnight

Pryce Williams

Lust

Envy

Home Before Midnight

Simeon King

So This is Love

Gluttony

Sloth

Rylee Daniels

Last Comes Love

Ready or Not
When Life Gives You Sunsets

Jaleel Gordon
Home for Christmas
Lust
Home Before Midnight

Alexis Hamilton
Rekindled
One Mic
Second Serving

Keith Aaron
Wrath
One Mic
Second Serving

book club questions

1. What was your first impression of Ivy Pressman?

2. What was your first impression of Leo Vanguard?

3. What were your thoughts about Ivy and Leo's early dynamic as friends before becoming guardians to Levi?

4. How did their friendship shift once they started raising Levi together? Did anything about that shift surprise you?

5. What do you think Ivy and Leo's biggest challenges were—individually and as co-guardians?

6. How did grief play a role in their growth and connection throughout the story?

7. Do you think Leo handled his feelings for Ivy well? Why or why not?

8. Do you feel Ivy's hesitation toward pursuing a romantic relationship with Leo was justified?

9. What moment between Ivy and Leo stood out to you the most? Why?

10. Who do you think grew the most by the end of the story—and in what way?